FATED TO THE ALIEN WARRIOR

WARRIORS OF TAVIKH

BOOK ONE

ERIN HALE

❀ Created with Vellum

CHAPTER 1

Maybe I should have let them throw me in prison.

My whole body shakes along with the spaceship I'm sitting in, and I clench my eyes closed even tighter. Against my will, a whimper escapes my pinched lips.

"Man, I didn't know a person could turn that shade of green. You're not going to hork everywhere, are you?"

I slit one eye open and peek out of it to glare at the woman seated across from me. Her expression is concerned, but there had been a tone of amusement in her question as well. Another rattle of the death trap makes me suck in a breath. I snap my eyelid closed. If this fucking ship is going to crash and kill us all, I don't want to see it coming.

"Hey," the woman says soothingly, "we're going to be fine. There's nothing to worry about. This is totally normal."

I latch onto the last part and repeat it silently in my head. *This is normal. It's normal. Everything is normal.* At last the shuddering stops, and the ride smooths out. It's still several minutes before I manage to slowly open my eyes. My fingers loosen their white-knuckled grip on the arm rests. The organ inside my chest continues racing, but then it, too, returns to a regular beat.

"You look a little less sick. Feeling okay now?" the woman asks. She doesn't appear nervous at all.

I nod my head shakily. "Never better."

She barks out a laugh. "I'd hate to see you when you really feel like shit."

My lips tip up in a partial smile. It's the most I can accomplish at the moment. I glance around the interior of the cabin. Based on a few other people's expressions, it would seem I'm not the only one who's anxious about the rough start.

"I'm Remi, by the way."

I turn back to my new acquaintance, who doesn't appear to be much older than me. "London."

"First time heading to space I take it?" she asks.

"Yeah."

"Mine too."

I wiggle my fingers, which are still numb from the lack of blood. Seconds later, sensation returns to them. Overhead, the speaker crackles and a disembodied male voice comes through it.

"This is Captain Blanchard speaking. We have exited Earth's atmosphere and begun our flight to the planet, Tavikh. Staterooms and the dining hall are located on the second level. You will find a fitness room and passenger rec room on the main level. Crew members will be circulating through the ship if you have any questions. Otherwise, enjoy the trip." There's a short burst of static and then, silence.

That's it, I guess. For the next two months, I'm stuck inside this hulking tin can full of strangers, on our way to some new planet where we're expected to work the small patch of land we've been given for the rest of our miserable lives. Shit, I should have just picked prison. At least I'd still be on Earth where everything is familiar.

"You okay?" Remi asks, shaking me out of my thoughts.

"Hmm? Oh, yep, just peachy." I bite back a wince at my sarcasm. She's only trying to be nice. "Sorry. I'm fine, thanks."

"I don't know about you, but there's no way I'm going to be able to sit here and do nothing for much longer. You up for a little bit of exploring?"

Exploring? As in take off my safety belt and wander around this giant heap of metal that is taking me away from everything I've ever known? Not that it's been that great, but better the devil I know.

"C'mon," Remi coaxes, already rising to her feet. "It'll do you good to move around and get your mind on something besides being nervous. Personally, I want to check out the training room."

The fact that she's probably right chafes a bit, but I let loose a sigh and unhook the straps over my chest, holding me in place. I'm a bit unsteady, but I manage to gather my space legs and sweep my arm out. "Lead the way."

We walk through the main cabin, passing an array of people ranging from other women our age to couples and families with children to even several older men and women. All of us—for one reason or another—venturing to a whole new world. I glance at Remi's back as she guides us out and into a slightly curved metal hallway, its dark material barely illuminated by the soft ambient light of evenly spaced bulbs recessed in the ceiling.

I'd ask her why she's on her way to Tavikh, but that will open up a conversation I don't particularly want to have. I have no plans to tell anyone that I'm nothing more than a common thief. And not even a good one at that, considering my mark caught me. The court sentenced me to either spend fifty years in an overly populated prison full of criminals far more dangerous than me or get shipped off to another planet.

I should have picked prison. Except it's too late for that. Tavikh is my new life. My do-over. My way to become someone different from who I've been the last twenty-seven years. I can make something of myself. My gaze lands on Remi. I can have friends. I can make my mother proud.

As though sensing my eyes on her, Remi glances over her shoulder. "You okay back there? You have this weird expression on your face."

"Yeah, I'm good."

We continue trekking down the hallway, passing the occasional crew member wearing their dark red uniform with insignia stitched on the left chest. Our footsteps echo in the cavernous metallic space. We pass several recessed stairwells that lead, I assume, up to the second floor where the captain had explained the cafeteria and our rooms were located.

At last, Remi and I reach a set of open double doors. We peek inside. A running track lines the perimeter of a room the size of those old high school gymnasiums I've seen on vids. Left of center, two crewmen grapple on a mat, both of them intent and focused on each other. Otherwise, the room is empty of people.

There are some weights off to one side, and dangling from the ceiling above several more mats are two thick ropes, about six or seven feet apart.

"I'm definitely coming back later," Remi remarks, her gaze assessing one of the ropes as though contemplating scaling it. She doesn't look like she'd have the strength to haul herself all the way to the top, but then again, what do I know?

She turns to me. "Do you know what cabin you're in?"

Shit. Think. Oh yeah. "Fifteen-oh-one."

"No way. I'm fifteen-oh-three. We might be neighbors. Let's check out the second floor and find where we're going to be sleeping for the next two months."

Apparently, Remi has decided she's the leader of our little twosome, which is fine by me. I've always been a follower anyway. *Keep quiet. Do what you're told.* It's always worked for me in the past. Or it did until I wound up arrested.

Back out in the hallway, we climb a set of stairs and reach the upper level. It's a mirror image of the bottom level, except on one side of the wall are doors, each one with a numbered metal placard and bioscanner to the right of it. We roam the hall until, at last, we come across Remi's room and, two doors down, mine.

She places her palm on the scanner outside her room and the door slides open with a soft whoosh. She disappears inside. I close the distance and stand in the doorway. The room is utilitarian, with a double-sized bunk bed against one wall, a six-drawer rectangular dresser on another, and a small table with two chairs slightly off to the side. There's a single door at the back that I assume leads to the washroom.

Remi plunks down on the bottom bunk and pats the mattress on either side of her hips. "Not the softest bed I've ever slept in, but I guess it'll do."

My stomach rumbles, and I flush. I'd been too nervous to eat before boarding.

"Didn't the guy over the speaker say the cafeteria was on this level? Maybe they have snacks," she says, rising from the bed.

Once again, I trail behind her until finally, we come to the cafeteria. Long tables flanked by a backless bench on either side are spread throughout. Toward the back is a stack of trays and several food replicators. Remi strides across the room and pauses in front of one of them.

"What do you fancy?" she calls over her shoulder.

"Cheeseburger and french fries," I answer without hesitation, shortening the distance until I stand next to her. My mouth is already watering. It's the one meal I've always wanted to have, but my mother could never afford, no matter how much work she did to try and barter for food.

Remi nods and presses a couple buttons. "Coming right up."

I grab a tray just as my stomach rumbles again. Weird hissing noises come from the replicator until the red light above the door switches to green and the machine beeps. A metal section slides up and she reaches inside, the scent of cooked meat wafting from it. It smells exactly how I always pictured it would. She pulls out a plate and sets it on my tray. On it is the biggest cheeseburger I've ever seen, with fries nearly falling over the edge of the dish.

A part of me wants to shove the whole thing in my mouth, but I wait for Remi while she presses a couple more buttons for whatever she's eating. My finger taps the corner of my tray in an impatient beat.

"Looks like someone else had the same idea," a new feminine voice comes from behind me.

Remi and I turn to find a petite blonde with a huge grin walking toward us. "I'm not intruding am I?" she asks.

"No, not at all," Remi says. "We're just grabbing a quick bite."

"Do you mind if I join you?"

Remi glances at me and I nod. "Sure."

"Excellent. I'm Zara by the way."

"Remi." She gestures toward me with a thumb. "And this is London."

"Pleased to meet you." Zara pushes the buttons on one of the other replicators, and in only a couple minutes, the three of us are seated at one of the tables.

I measure my bites, not wanting to seem desperate for food. Plus, I want to savor the juicy burger and crisp cut potatoes. Make them last. It's not as though I can't get another at the next meal, but this first one is special and perfect.

"Either of you ever been to space before?" Zara asks between bites.

Remi and I shake our heads.

"Oh boy, are you in for a treat. It's like nothing you've ever seen," she tells us. "You don't know what dark is until you've glanced out a window into the absolute nothingness of space. Especially when there aren't any stars out there. It's freaky as hell."

The nausea from takeoff returns and I swallow hard then guzzle down my glass of water. It sounds fucking terrifying. Remi must see something on my face, because she nudges my foot under the table and sends me a reassuring smile. I'm grateful for it.

"So, Zara, what takes you to Tavikh?" Remi asks.

The other woman shrugs, but there's a tightness around her mouth and eyes. "Change of scenery, I guess. You know how it is."

Silence settles between us. It would seem that no one is keen to share the actual reason she's on this ship. Soon we each finish our meal. I'm stuffed, and the sleep I didn't get last night is catching up with me. I stifle a yawn. "If you guys don't mind, I think I'm going to head to my room for a little bit. Lie down. Maybe take a nap."

"Sounds like a plan," Remi says.

The three of us dump our trays and head back down the hall toward our rooms. We reach mine first.

"It was…nice meeting you, Zara," I tell her, trying to be polite. I've never been good at making friends.

"You as well. It also looks like we're neighbors. That's my room." She nods at the door between Remi's and mine.

"And I'm on the other side of that," Remi adds.

Zara's gaze bounces between us and her toothy smile is wide and blinding. "I hope this means we'll get to be friends on the trip."

"That'll be nice," I manage. "I guess I'll see you guys later."

The two of them wave. I place my hand on the bioscanner. The door opens with a swoosh, and a light automatically turns on. I step inside. The layout is identical to Remi's room. On the bottom bunk is my tattered bag containing all my worldly possessions. An actual suitcase sits on the top bunk. The crew must have brought everyone's belongings to their rooms, since I'd left mine where I'd been instructed to outside the ship.

I explore the room, although there isn't much to it. In the washroom is a toilet, sink, and shower. There's also a small shelf with a few towels. I turn off the light and plop down on the bottom bunk, nudging my sack out of the way. Then, I curl up on my side and tuck my hands under my cheek.

The pillowcase is slightly scratchy against my skin, but this small room is better than where I've been sleeping for the last two months since…well, since. My eyes close and I take a deep breath. A tear leaks out and drips down my temple before disappearing into my hair.

I'm all alone. No one is left. And this…whatever it is, is my life. Lying here—in a spaceship—bound for a planet in a far-off place with everything I own in a tiny bag at the foot of my bed. Tomorrow I'll make the best of things. Plan for a better future. But until then, I'm mourning all that I've lost. Even if it hadn't been much.

CHAPTER 2

The whooshing sound of the door jerks my eyes open. I must have dozed, because, for a second, I'm disoriented and not sure where I am. *How long have I been lying here?*

"I'm sorry, I didn't realize anyone was in here already," the woman in the doorway says.

I quickly sit up and brush back the hair covering half my face. "It's okay. Hi, um, I'm London. I guess we must be roommates."

She slowly steps inside, and the door closes behind her. She remains standing, almost in the middle of the room, with her arms wrapped around her waist. I can't tell if she's cold or if it's a protective gesture, which seems weird. It's not like I'm going to hurt her. And something about the pose makes her appear younger, almost vulnerable.

"Maeve," she finally says, her voice soft and barely audible.

"It's nice to meet you." Smiling comes a bit easier. I must be getting a hang of this friend thing. "My bag was already on this bed, but if you'd rather have it, I'll take the top one."

Maeve shakes her head, her short, straight brown hair barely grazing her jaw. "No, it's fine."

A heavy and awkward silence falls as her gaze lands everywhere but on me. *Shit, I thought I was doing so well. Where's Remi when I need her?* "Um, would you like to unpack your things? You have first dibs on which side of the dresser you want. I haven't put anything in there yet."

Finally, Maeve moves. She pulls her suitcase down quietly and sets it on top of the dresser. I stay where I'm at. Anything to not make this more uncomfortable than it already is. In no time, she's finished.

"You can slide your empty luggage under the bunk if you want. I promise I won't bother it," I tell her as I stand and move out of her way.

With only a second's hesitation, she squats and pushes it underneath before rising. "Thanks."

"No problem. So, is this your first time in space? It is mine, and I thought I was going to barf before we even made it through the outer atmosphere," I babble without taking a breath.

Maeve actually cracks a slight smile. "Me too. I hadn't expected so much shaking."

"Oh my god, it was the worst. I'm glad it didn't last long. I would have horribly embarrassed myself," I admit. "You can have a seat if you want."

"Thanks."

We both move toward the small table at the same time. Maeve jumps away from me. I freeze. *What the hell*? Her face flushes. She takes in a shuddering breath and continues heading to the chairs, as though nothing just happened, before quickly lowering herself into one. I take a cautious step forward and then another and another until I reach the second, surprisingly soft, chair. A few seconds of awkward silence surrounds us until, finally, Maeve seems to lower her guard a fraction.

"Have you been anywhere else on the ship yet?" she asks.

"My friend Remi and I did a little exploring shortly after takeoff," I tell her. "We scouted out what they called the training room. I'm not really athletic, so I don't think I'll get much use out of it, but Remi seemed excited about being in there. Then we ate in the cafeteria. I must have fallen asleep when I got back here, so I'm not sure how long ago that was. Oh, and we met another woman about our age. Zara. Her room is actually next door, and Remi is on the other side of her."

"Did you and Remi come together?" Maeve asks.

I shake my head with a little laugh. "Oh, no, she sort of adopted me, I guess. We were sitting across from each other during takeoff. Pretty sure she was afraid I was going to throw up all over her."

Maeve chuckles. "I'm sure she's glad you didn't."

"No more than I am." I pause and debate on bringing it up. Better just to get it out in the open first. "I take it you're going to Tavikh for a…change of scenery like the rest of us?"

An expression flashes across her face so quickly I nearly miss it, but I could swear it's fear. Then it's gone, and in its place is a blank mask. "Something like that."

"I promise I won't pry," I rush to assure her. "Whatever reasons you have are your own."

Maeve nods shallowly but doesn't say anything else. Her whole body almost shrinks in on itself as though she's trying to make herself seem smaller until she could disappear. *Great job, London. Scare away only the third friend you even have.*

I clear my throat and try to bring back the easy conversation we had going on before I ruined it. "If you want, I can show you around the ship. Maybe we can find the passenger rec room the captain mentioned. Remi and I missed it during our search."

Maeve doesn't respond for several seconds, as though weighing her decision. "That would be nice."

"Great."

Yet again, I find myself walking around—this time in the lead—and pointing out the cafeteria on this floor and the training room down below. We pass a ton of other passengers exploring like us. I assume they, too, are orienting themselves to the place. Beside me, Maeve jumps the tiniest bit every time someone comes around the bend. She moves incrementally closer, with her head down, keeping me between her and anyone who walks by. I don't question why.

At last, we manage to find the rec room. I walk through the door and gasp. "Oh my god, they have books?"

There aren't many—only a single bookcase—but the fact they have any at all almost makes me cry. All forms of media have been moved to datapads, something neither my mother nor I had been able to afford, and physical books are nearly impossible to find anymore.

When I was little, she used to read to me from the one or two she still managed to own. They were fairytale adventures of this young girl and the magical quest she was on. I nearly rush across the room, but instead, keep my pace even until I reach the case. My fingers gently trace the spines of each and every book on the shelves. They seem to be mostly mysteries and thrillers, but there are also a couple biographies and a few children's books. I even spot some historical Westerns.

I pull one off the shelf, open the pages, and breathe in the scent of the yellowed paper. It reminds me of my mother, and I sniff back the tears. I miss her so much. Carefully, I return it to its place. I'll come back soon when I'm alone and pick one out to borrow.

"Look, they have Pebbles." Maeve says from her spot on the other side of the room. She's standing next to a small table with games stacked on it.

"What's that?"

Her eyes widen. "You don't know what Pebbles is?"

A flush rises up my neck and cheeks and I shake my head. Something like pity crosses her face.

"It's a game I used to play all the time when I was a kid. I can teach you if you'd like. It'll be something fun to do to pass the time. Maybe your other friends can join us," she offers.

I nod, still embarrassed that I don't know what some stupid children's game is. "I'm sure they'd enjoy it."

"I'm actually starting to get hungry," Maeve says. "I think I'm going to head back to the cafeteria and get some food. Do you want to come with?"

My gaze lands on the books and then returns to her. "You go ahead. I'm going to pick out something to read."

"Ok—okay." Something like panic flashes across her face. "I, um, guess I'll see you back at the room."

For several minutes after she's gone, I continue standing there. My gaze takes in the rest of the room, and I spot several comfortable couches. I wander around and pick up one of the datapads. Out of curiosity, I power it on. The screen lights up and shows the outline of a head. I hold it in front of my face.

There's a quiet beep and then my name pops up, along with my cabin number. The screen switches again and a main menu displays. There are books, magazines, newspapers, and a whole catalog of vids I can choose from, ranging from comedies to action to…wait, is that porn?

I quickly shut the device off and stash it back where it came from. My face heats. I'll stick with real books for the moment. I move to the table where Maeve found the game she called Pebbles. I open the small, labeled box and stare at its contents. There are literally only five smooth stones inside, each no bigger than a couple inches around. This is a kid's game? What the hell do you do with them? I close the lid and set it back down.

Unable to resist any longer, I return to the bookcase and scan the offerings until finally deciding on a Western. My mother imbued her love of Earth's history on me. Those long ago days when cowboys roamed the land on their horses while they herded cattle and were a law unto themselves. It's a time and place I can't even imagine.

These days, every inch of Earth is overpopulated. Corporations have built up all the land and placed their skyscrapers and apartment buildings nearly on top of each other. No longer do fields exist where animals roamed. Instead, all our food is manufactured with replicators. At least for those who can afford to own one. The rest of us have survived on protein bars.

It's actually the one thing I'm looking forward to on Tavikh. Being able to grow my own fruits and vegetables. There will be real, genuine farmland. Maybe some of the residents will find some animals to hunt for meat.

Although, we'll probably just fuck it up all over again. I can't worry about that yet. I'll just take one day at a time.

I curl up on the end of one of the couches and open the book, taking care not to crease the spine more than it already is. Soon, I'm engrossed in an engaging story of much simpler times but filled with enough action and adventure to keep me entertained.

My mother would have loved this story. I take pleasure in that knowledge even if she can't be here to share it with me. What would she think of me heading off to space? Would she be disappointed in the choices I've made? I'm glad she isn't alive to see how far I've fallen since she's been gone.

CHAPTER 3

These humans are going to get themselves killed. I stand within the shadows cast by the trees at the edge of the forest as the small group of males traipses through the field, not bothering to soften their steps or quiet their voices.

"Do the humans *want* to die?" my younger brother Zydon echoes my thoughts, his voice barely a whisper over the soft breeze that floats by.

"I don't think that's their intent. But their skills of the hunt are sorely lacking. They don't know the meaning of stealth." I shake my head.

They also don't want our assistance, no matter how many times we've offered. In fact, the hostility that has greeted us whenever we approach the human settlement has curbed our desire to bother anymore. Still, we have no wish for innocents to be killed. So we stand by—observing —in case trouble arises. As they're coming to discover, beings far more dangerous than these humans could ever imagine inhabit our planet.

Zydon scoffs. "They're like kits fumbling around on their first hunt. I don't think they will ever learn. It's almost as though they just expect the dreri to fall dead at their feet."

I can't help but chuckle. My brother isn't wrong. Although none of the kits back in our village are as careless as this small group of human males.

"Did you hear that another ship carrying more humans arrives soon?" Zydon asks, his tone scornful.

I jerk my head in his direction. "What?"

"Jodah was out hunting for leburin and stumbled across their two tribe leaders outside the settlement walls. Over-heard them discussing it."

"How soon?" I ask.

"Less than three turns of the sun. Maybe even before then."

Over the last six lunar cycles, several ships have landed on Tavikh, each one carrying fifty to a hundred passengers. They've settled in a small village built twelve lunar cycles ago when the first group landed. At first, we'd been curious about these new arrivals. But the more that have been delivered, the more problems that have arisen.

Especially because with each new ship, the attacks by the Krijese have escalated. Many humans have died, despite our efforts to protect them from our enemies. Yet ships continue to land here as though the human leaders on Earth don't care what happens to the passengers once they've arrived. As though they are expendable.

"Look." Zydon points along the horizon.

A pair of dreri have ventured into the far side of the field, upwind of the clumsy humans. In only moments, one of the hunters spots the prey. He slowly makes his way closer to them, the spear in his hand raised to strike. I continue watching as the male stalks forward.

He throws his weapon at the nearest dreri and misses. The two animals scatter with long, loping jumps, and soon disappear in the distance. The human curses and kicks the ground, as though blaming it for his inadequacies. The group turns and heads back toward the settlement, seeming to have already given up for the day.

Once again, I shake my head. "Come, let us return to the village."

We enter the forest behind us, the familiar scent of trendafili and nenuphar filling the air. The trees provide a canopy against the heat of the sun. As we navigate the path back to our home, a sense of unease works its way into my belly. Over time, I've learned to listen to it, despite not understanding what causes it or what it's telling me until something happens.

Our planet is changing with the arrival of the humans. Their people have started to invade some of the best hunting regions. How soon until they no longer want to share the land with us?

As tribe leader, it's up to me to protect our people. We're already at war with the Krijese, and there's an unsteady acceptance between my tribe and the human's. I have no desire to make any more enemies.

Shaking off the unpleasant thoughts of things that may not ever come to be, I turn my attention back to my surroundings and any dangers that might lurk in the shadows. Soon, Zydon and I cross the border of our territory. No doubt the scouts already sent word of our arrival.

Not long after, the scent of the evening fire reaches me, along with the mouth-watering aroma of fresh-cooked meat. The two guards stationed at the entrance greet us with fists over their chests.

"Shefir," they address me.

I nod as I pass. The chatter of voices and the laughter of kits brings a smile to my face. Young males and females run happily through the village, weaving around tents and tribe members as they play. For a moment, a pang of want hits me.

Mated and unmated females cluster around the fire preparing the evening meal, while several males stride through the village, most likely to put away their weapons after a day of hunting and scouting. Others carry their kills toward the tanning tent where they will be cleaned and prepared for tomorrow's meal.

"I'm going to find Jodah and discuss our next hunt," Zydon says and claps my shoulder before he heads in the opposite direction.

I make my way toward my own tent for a moment's peace before the evening meal begins.

"Zander," a male calls out.

My gaze lands on Benham, our tribe's lead warrior and weapons craftsman, heading my way. He stops in front of me and crosses his fist over his chest before lowering it.

"It would seem the bounty was plentiful today," I note, returning the gesture of respect.

He nods, his expression as serious as always. "Yes, the hunters have returned with enough food to last for several turns of the moons."

"Excellent." I smile with pride.

"We did run across a problem though," Benham says. "A half turn of the sun's walk from here, we came across the bodies of several dead male humans. The shkaba were picking at their remains."

"Fuck. How did they die?"

"The Krijese." An expression of rage crosses his face. "We gave them a proper burial."

I curse again. Not only are our enemies attacking the human settlement, but it would seem as though they're hunting them outside of it as well. Tomorrow I will need to warn their tribe's leaders to take extra precautions when leaving their border walls. However, if past experience has told me anything, they will not welcome my presence.

"Our enemies are getting bolder," Benham says. "They have moved increasingly closer to our territory. It doesn't help that the humans have made their home directly in the lands between ours. The Krijese are no doubt making plans on how to take it from them. They've been encroaching on the neutral territory for many lunar cycles already."

"We won't let that happen," I growl. "Gather a few warriors after the meal and assign extra patrols near the human's encampment. I will join you tomorrow and attempt to speak with their tribe leaders."

Benham snorts. "I don't envy you. Never before have I seen such carelessness as with the humans. They don't want to listen to us or our warnings. Stubborn fools."

"That may be, but we must do what we can to protect them," I say gravely.

He merely shakes his head. "Our warriors will follow your orders, even if the foolish humans don't appreciate our presence. I don't know if they're merely naive or willfully ignorant of the dangers."

"Perhaps a little of both." I smile. "If there's nothing else?"

Benham shakes his head. "That is all."

I clap his shoulder and once again make my way to my tent. Aside from the healer's, it is the largest in the village and sits near the back, slightly apart from the rest. I push open the flap and step inside. Already, someone has lit the fire in the center in preparation for my arrival.

The welcoming scent of livando lingers in the air from the small bundles that dangle from the wooden supports. It's the one thing from being a kit I can't seem to let go of. The scent reminds me of growing up, before my nene's death. I cross the space and rinse my hands in the basin of water that is set on the low table beside my pallet of furs.

I splash some on my face and upper body to rinse off the yellowish dust of the land the wind kicks up, which often clings to our leathered skin. Once I'm clean enough, I dry myself with a nearby cloth before tossing it onto the table. The faded sounds of village life filter through the hide of my home, reminding me of how quiet it is inside.

There's no mate to greet me with a warm touch. To fuss over me after a long day of hunting. To sit around the fire and eat with me. Or talk with me. Or to warm my furs at night. There are a couple females who would love to become my Shefira, but none of them hold my interest. None of them have ever caused the mating marks that line my skin to burn or flare with color. I worry none of them ever will.

Taking a deep breath and releasing it on a heavy sigh, I exit my tent, trying to push away the unsettled feeling that seems to grow stronger with each turn of the sun. Instead, I paste an easy expression on my face and move to join the rest of the village at the main fire for the evening meal. I have more than enough to worry about with keeping our village prosperous and protecting not only them but the humans, without adding the restless feeling of being without a mate.

"Shefir, Shefir," one of the kits calls out for me the moment I step out of my tent. Talek runs forward and nearly crashes into my legs. "Will you tell us the story again about how, when you were our age, you spent three turns of the sun stalking the luani, and how you killed it with only a single blade?"

"Just a blade, huh? Is that what happened?" Zydon asks, approaching us with a raised brow and smirk.

I laugh at the kit's enthusiasm and shoot my brother a dirty look. Perhaps there might have been a slight exaggeration made to the events that actually happened—like the fact that I'd only gotten in the kill by accident when I fell out of the tree I'd fallen asleep in and landed on top of the already nearly dead and elderly beast. But all the kits enjoy the story and frequently ask for its retelling.

"After the evening meal, I'll share the story again." I brush my hand over Talek's head, another wave of emotion sparking inside me.

"Thank you, Shefir," he says with a giant grin and darts away to join a small group of young males.

For a moment I stand and watch them run around, laughing and enjoying themselves. A memory flashes of Zydon, Zedam, and me as kits. The three of us fighting with small wooden swords our baba had made for us.

Pain stabs my chest. Baba is gone. Nene too. After she died, his spirit died with her until, far too soon, his body joined hers in the land of the goddess, Deeka. Their souls were too intertwined, and the pain and suffering too great to survive long after the death of their mate.

"He's still alive," Zydon says gruffly. "Somewhere. We'll find him."

I glance at my brother, not surprised by his words. He always knows what I'm thinking. Perhaps it is due to the fact we shared our nene's womb.

"There was blood. As well as his sword," I remind him. "Zedam would never have left it otherwise."

"Unless he had no other choice," Zydon says gravely. "We *will* find him."

The thought of our youngest brother's death nearly takes my breath. Our baba had Benham make each of us our own weapon designed specifically for us. None of us would ever be parted from ours. Except by death.

The weight of responsibility weighs heavy on my shoulders. I've never regretted inheriting my position after Baba's death, but there are times where I wish I had someone to share my burdens with. My brother means well, but he's far too impulsive.

"Come, let us eat and gather our energy for tomorrow. We're going to need it," I tell him.

Without waiting for Zydon to follow, I cross the length of the village toward the central fire, my thoughts a swirling storm that doesn't seem to want to settle. But, as I told my brother, tomorrow will be here soon and we'll have a different set of problems to deal with.

CHAPTER 4

Any moment we'll finally be landing on Tavikh. The same nausea that had plagued me during takeoff those two long months ago returned in full force when I woke up this morning, and it hasn't left yet. Remi, Zara, and Maeve have done everything they can to take my mind off our upcoming arrival.

"You are such a dirty cheat," Remi barks through her laughter. Even quiet Maeve joins in.

Zara raises her hands in surrender, three shiny rocks nearly falling out of her palm. "As if I would ever do that."

Maeve coughs but tries to cover it up. Remi points at her. "See, even Maeve knows you're full of shit. Just because London and I hadn't played before this trip doesn't mean you get to make up new rules just so you win."

I shake my head at their antics. I'd been surprised to learn that Remi hadn't known how to play Pebbles either, which made me feel better. So, as promised, Maeve taught us. It still hasn't stopped Zara from bending the rules to her advantage when she thinks she can get away with it.

"Fine. Be a spoilsport." She puts the stones back on the floor and then it's my turn.

Wiggling my fingers to try and loosen them up, I pick up the first pebble. I toss it in the air, pick up a second stone, and then catch the first one in the same palm before it can hit the floor. They clink against each other. With only a short pause, I toss them both up together and snatch up a third before quickly catching the two falling ones so all three are nestled in my hand.

This is where I always fuck up. Taking a deep breath, I focus hard and roll the three stones to try and keep them tightly packed against each other. *Toss.* Almost before they're out of my hand I grab the fourth stone and desperately try to catch the other three.

One.

Two.

Thud.

"Son of a bitch." With an exasperated sigh, I drop the pebbles from my palm onto the floor to collide with the two lying there.

"You'll get it next time," Maeve encourages softly beside me.

I give her a grateful smile. "Thanks."

The familiar crackle of the overhead speaker draws our eyes to the ceiling. "This is Captain Blanchard speaking. We are about to enter the outer atmosphere of Tavikh. Please make your way to the passenger cabin and secure your safety belts. We'll be landing shortly."

My anxiety spikes, but I take several deep breaths. This is it. My fresh start with new friends and a whole new life that is waiting for me the moment we touch down. Things on Tavikh are going to be different than they were on Earth. Here I'll be free of everything that had been holding me back there. Poverty. Being alone.

"No horking this time," Remi says with an amused smile as she rises to her feet with the rest of us.

"Very funny," I growl, affronted. "You'll never let that go will you?"

"Nope," she says with a *pop*.

Maeve puts the pebbles back in their box and sets it on the table. The four of us head out into the hallway and toward the passenger cabin where we take the same seats we arrived in. I glance at Remi across from me and then my gaze travels a few people over to find Zara and Maeve. The latter sends me a shy smile.

"You ready?" Remi asks, her tone more serious than I can recall it being since we met.

I shake my head. "Not in the slightest. You?"

Her expression shifts to mischievous. "Are you kidding? This is the best adventure I've ever been on. I'm excited to see what this new planet has to offer. It has to be better than what I left behind."

This is the first time Remi—any of us, in fact—has mentioned her past life. It's unofficially been a closed topic for all of us. My burning curiosity wants me to probe deeper into what she means, but I keep my mouth closed. Maybe one of these days, we'll be ready to share with each other our reasons for coming to Tavikh.

"It will be," I agree. It has to be or what is the whole point?

The ship rattles and the familiar creaking grates on my nerves, stirring up the nausea in my belly. I keep my eyes on Remi and concentrate on my breathing. Her words from the first time we sat in these seats echo inside my head. *This is normal.*

She nods and smiles at me with giddy excitement, her eyes wide and expressive, like a little kid. Oddly, it helps to calm me. In fact, a flutter of a similar emotion to hers dances in my chest. The ship stops shaking and my tense muscles relax.

"Don't forget," Remi begins. "When we get there, I'm moving into the house next to yours. You're never going to get rid of me."

"Thanks for the warning." I chuckle.

A hard thump reverberates through my seat and my body jolts. "Damn, couldn't the captain have given us a softer landing?"

As though hearing my complaint, the overhead speaker emits a burst of static.

"Welcome to Tavikh. Please head toward the loading dock immediately and in an orderly fashion. Don't delay. Your bags will be off-loaded, transported into the settlement, and distributed from there. The minute you disembark, quickly make your way inside the gates and lock the doors." There's a brief pause. "Good luck."

When nothing further is said, I glance over at Remi. Had she noticed the tone of the captain's farewell? "That was… weird. Gates? Settlement? Good luck? I'm not sure I like how that sounded."

Her forehead wrinkles. "Yeah, that was a little creepy."

Zara and Maeve are suddenly in front of us, the former's expression a mirror of Remi's. "Jesus. Ominous much?"

Clearly it's not just us then. Remi and I stand and join our friends behind the crowd that is slowly exiting the cabin and heading toward the loading dock. Our steps are slow, and before I'm ready, we're there. A blinding sun shines from the sky, and I get my first look at Tavikh.

Beneath my feet, the ground is yellow, and the wind kicks up the dirt which seems to give everything a yellowish tint. In front of me is a field of shin-high grass, but it's unlike any grass I've ever seen. Not only does it appear soft and fluffy, it's also a brighter shade of yellow than the dirt.

A forest lays far beyond the field, but the trees don't resemble the few remaining ones on Earth or from any vids I've watched. Their trunks and branches appear black as night from here, while the leaves are a rich purple. My gaze narrows on a shadow beneath the looming foliage. It feels as though something inside the darkness there is watching me. I shiver at the unnerving sensation that creeps down my back.

"Holy shit," Remi breathes out from beside me. "Can you believe this place?"

"It's definitely not at all what I expected," I reply. Or what we were told.

"Where do you think—" Her words are cut short by an unholy roar that sends my heart plummeting into my stomach.

I swivel left and right, trying to pinpoint where the sound came from, when a scream reaches my ears. The hairs on my arm stand straight up.

"Run," someone yells.

Chaos ensues. People scatter in confusion. Remi grabs my hand and drags me away from the ship and toward the front gates of the settlement, which seem so far away. "Let's go."

My panicked gaze darts to her as my brain finally catches up. We both run, with Zara and Maeve right beside us.

My lungs burn and there's a stitch growing in my side. More animalistic growls fill the air, followed by human screams that are made far more terrifying by the fact that they abruptly cut off. I swear I feel hot breath ghosting along the back of my neck. My toe catches on something. I stumble and fall to my knees. Remi's hand is ripped from mine.

"London," she cries out.

Sharp pain bursts through my legs, and my palms sting from scraping across the hardened ground. Before I can suck in a breath, strong arms scoop me up and I'm thrown over the massive shoulder of someone who takes off running. The hard angles dig into my stomach with each bouncing movement, so much that I can't even scream. My head dangles toward the yellow dirt, the sight of it partially obscured by the curtain of my hair. *Where are they taking me?*

As though drawing on some unknown strength, I manage to inhale and let it out on a violent screech. My legs kick and I punch and claw at my captor. A large hand clamps down on the back of my thighs, far too close to my lady bits I draw in a sharp breath and freeze.

Seconds later, I'm airborne and then landing on my feet. I would have fallen over if someone hadn't steadied me. My gaze darts up, and up even further. My eyes widen as they latch onto another pair, completely different—otherworldly—than mine and my mouth gapes. I can't form words. I can barely breathe. Standing in front of me is a fucking alien. A huge, *purple* alien with yellowish eyes and long, flowing golden hair. Weird marks on his skin, like tattoos, brighten in color and turn a deeper purple than the rest of him.

"Oh my god." Zara's voice—*I think it's hers*—comes from my left.

His gaze glides down my body before he blinks and spins away. My eyes bug. *Holy shit, he has a tail.* He takes off running, sword in hand, and joins a group of men—aliens—who look similar to him, as they battle another group of aliens. Horrific, terrifying ones with dark hair that dances and swirls and reminds me of a pit of snakes. A vertical line splits the lower half of their faces and folds open to display a mouthful of razor-sharp teeth. Their ugliness is a stark contrast to the almost ethereal beauty of the one who'd carried me away.

"Christ on a cracker. London, are you okay?"

It takes everything I have to tear my gaze away from the fighting taking place only feet from me and turn to Remi. She, Zara, and Maeve surround me. We're inside the settlement walls and it's madness. Bodies—human and alien—lie scattered on the ground, while other people are helping those that appear to be injured.

I nod, my head bobbing with a jerky motion. "Ye—yeah, I think so."

Somebody's closed the gates, keeping us trapped in here with…aliens. Their powerful bodies move with fluid ease despite the ferocity they show. One by one, the dark-haired ones fall, until only the white gold—haired, purple ones remain standing.

Women and children are crying. Men rush around, their voices harsh and grating as they bark out commands. My feet remain planted where they are, as though I'm paralyzed. My friends' breaths are loud, but they barely register over my own. I'm shaking and cold. Colder than

I've ever been before. Even on the nights when I lay huddled in a darkened alley with nothing more than a thin blanket to cover me.

Maeve. My worried gaze darts to her. From the moment we met, she's been skittish. Always jumping at shadows. Her face is a blank white sheet, and there's a glassy look in her eyes. Like she's not even seeing anything.

"Maeve," I call her name softly, trying not to startle her. "Hey, it's London."

She blinks, meets my gaze, and wraps her arms around herself in a gesture I've come to realize is definitely protective. Her whole body trembles, but she nods briefly and seems to pull herself together. *Just.*

I glance back out over the settling melee. The same alien who'd carried me into the settlement turns. Our eyes meet. There's ringing in my ears and all the sounds echoing around me fade to a dull buzz. He slowly closes the distance between us and comes to a stop within an arm's length.

His face is almost humanoid, but there are enough differences to make it obvious he's an alien. Like the hard ridges where eyebrows should be. The vertical pupils like a feline. And the flat, bony nose. A green liquid—blood?—covers his flesh, but a soft floral scent emanates from him. His yellow eyes brighten, and those marks on his skin darken further, flaring to an even deeper purple that's nearly black.

A loud *whoosh* fills my head, and then all the voices around me return, including Remi's.

"Who the fuck are you? And who the *fuck* were those guys?" She points at one of the dead aliens.

"I am Zander, Shefir of the Tavikhi. Those are our enemies, the Krijese." His deep voice rumbles over me and settles deep inside my belly, heating it from the inside out. Those mesmerizing eyes of his never leave mine.

Shefir? What does that mean? Then the rest of his words, or rather his language, penetrates my brain. "How can I understand you? You're not speaking English."

He nods. "I am not. I believe you humans have received translators that allow you to understand our language."

"Translators? I've never received a translator," I insist.

This *Zander* merely shrugs, an entirely too human gesture. "I do not know about your human technology. I only repeat what I have been told by your tribe leaders."

Every word out of this alien's mouth makes no sense. "How can you understand me then?"

He smirks and taps his ear. "My translator is capable of learning languages. The more I hear someone speak it, the more I understand it."

As though overwhelmed and overstimulated with all that's happening, my body sags. His strong hands catch me before I fall. A surge of awareness rises inside me at Zander's touch. *What is wrong with me*? Uncomfortable with the sensation, I take a sharp step away. One of my friends steadies me.

"I'm fine." I wave them off despite the quiver in my voice. I strengthen my tone. "I'm fine."

Zander's expression clouds but quickly clears as he separates the distance between us. But only by a fraction. He studies me, a slight cock to his head, as though he doesn't quite know what to make of me. "If you are all right, I need to speak with your tribe leaders about what occurred today."

I don't know who he's referring to as tribe leaders, but if it means he goes somewhere else, then I'm all for it. He...*unsettles* me in a way no one ever has before.

"I'm good," I rush to assure him.

He hesitates a moment before he crosses a fist over his chest, gives me a brief nod, and then walks away. At last I manage to pull in a full breath. A prickle of awareness heats the back of my neck. I turn and glance at my friends, who are all staring at me in wide-eyed wonder.

I shift self-consciously. "What?"

Remi's eyes bug even wider. "What do you mean *what*? Did you not see how that guy was looking at you? My god, I almost spontaneously combusted, and it wasn't even me he was watching. Girl, he is into you."

My face flares and I glance around, making sure no one heard her. She hadn't lowered her voice at all. I shake my head. "No he isn't. I mean, he's an alien. I'm human. Speaking of which, how come no one fucking told us there were aliens on this planet? Including ones who looked like they were trying to kill us?"

"I don't know," Zara says. "But I'm officially freaked the fuck out."

She isn't the only one. We've all been aware for years that aliens exist. Hell, our government has peace agreements with several different races. But I've never had a personal encounter with any before today. I glance back at Remi. There's a wild look in her eyes, but otherwise, her expression is relaxed. As usual, she seems to rally and take over the leadership role. Which is fine by me.

"Freaked out or not, this is our new home, and we can't just keep standing here doing nothing. Let's see what we can do to help."

The rest of us glance at each other and nod. She's right. Then we head over to a small cluster of people who seem to be giving out tasks. I'll do whatever I can to get the vision of a certain alien out of my mind.

CHAPTER 5

ZANDER

It's her.

Somehow, this tiny female is my mate. What is Deeka thinking giving me not only a human mate, but one who appears wary of me? How is this possible? Is this some sort of test of my worthiness as Shefir?

My gaze frequently darts to her, keeping a watchful eye to make sure she's in no danger. The Krijese have been killed, but I don't trust the human males to keep her safe. Not after all the death and destruction I've witnessed under their poor leadership.

I can't help but admire how lovely she is, with her long dark hair and tiny but curvy body. Her bright eyes remind me of the nenuphar plant, with its colorful petals and sweet fragrance. The top of her head barely reaches my shoulders. My fingers twitch with remembrance of her softness beneath their touch while I carried her.

Just seeing her makes the mating marks on my skin tingle and burn with pleasure. After all this time, Deeka has finally graced me with a mate.

"The bodies are ready to be moved, Shefir," a young warrior, Djale, says, his eyes widening as his gaze travels over me.

I ignore his unspoken question and instead focus on the situation at hand. The dead Krijese have been loaded onto three different sleds and will be taken to the edge of our enemy's territory and left for their tribe, to serve as a warning. The humans are under our protection, and this is the consequence of attacking them.

The Krijese won't heed our warning, of course. They will continue to bring war to my people—and the humans. It's in their blood, and they won't stop until they've all been destroyed.

"Thank you, Djale. And what of our own warriors? Any casualties?"

He shakes his head. "No, Shefir. A few minor injuries here and there, but nothing life-threatening."

Relief spreads through me at the news. Despite our skill with fighting, the Krijese are still extremely dangerous. "Good. Please coordinate with Benham and have three teams of two warriors each take the dead back to their lands."

He crosses a fist over his chest and hurries away. My gaze travels through the human settlement and lands on its two tribe leaders. I quickly close the distance between us. Their heads tip back to stare up at me, their eyes full of mistrust and trepidation.

"How many of your tribe members were killed today?" I ask bluntly.

They dart glances between each other and hesitate to answer. Finally, the slightly older of the two clears his throat. "Ten of them."

I curse. "How many total is that now? Fifty? Sixty? Your numbers dwindle with each new ship's arrival, and you refuse our offers of help. How many more of your people have to die before you accept it?"

Knowing my mate will reside within these walls only spurs my anger. I will do everything I can to protect her. Even if that means taking her from here and bringing her back to our village where I know she'll be safe.

The two males share another look and sigh in resignation. "What do you propose?"

"We will teach your warriors how to fight. How to hunt. How to protect your tribe from the Krijese."

The younger one shakes his head. "We aren't warriors."

"Then you will become warriors," I tell him fiercely. "Otherwise, your people will continue to die."

He nods. "We'll do what you say."

"You have made a wise decision. I will leave a few of our males here to get things settled. We will then return in the morning to begin your lessons." Without another word, I turn and walk away. I need to check on my mate.

As I move through the settlement, my gaze searches for her. The gates have been reopened and several of my warriors travel in and out, carrying supplies from the human's space craft. Another stands guard at the entrance, vigilant in his duty, watching for more Krijese.

Then, she walks through the opening, carrying several small metal boxes stacked on top of each other, and makes her way to a narrow building to the left. Not wanting to startle her, I make more noise than I typically do as I close the distance between us. Still, she jolts at the sight of me, her eyes widening slightly, and picks up her pace as though she can't get away fast enough.

I smile, an expression that doesn't come easy to me, to try and ease her fear, and raise my hands in an innocent gesture. She glances around, but no one is paying her any attention. They are all focused on their own tasks.

"Am I truly that terrifying?" I ask softly as I get close to her. "I mean you no harm, tiny human."

Her nose wrinkles. "I'm not tiny."

I smother my laugh at her indignant tone. Instead, I merely shrug. "You are to me."

We reach the door of the building. She juggles the burden in her arms and attempts to open it.

"Allow me." I grasp its handle and pull.

She glances up at me, still uncertain. "Thanks."

"Of course." I would offer to carry the items for her, but a voice in the back of my head tells me she will not appreciate it.

I follow her inside, keeping the door open, as she places the items on a shelf. I enjoy watching her. "What is your name?"

She narrows her gaze. "Why do you want to know?"

So suspicious, my little mate. "If we are going to live in villages near to each other, is it not common to know what to call someone? You know my name. Is it not fair for me to know yours as well?"

There's a lingering silence before she finally speaks. "London."

"London." I roll the name across my tongue, savoring its sound. "It is a beautiful name." As beautiful as the one who owns it.

Again, she stares at me with something like trepidation. I do my best to keep my expression loose and friendly, despite the growing arousal I'm feeling at being in this enclosed space with her, where her fragrance surrounds me. Calls to me. She smells of the lulebore bush. It is a pleasing scent.

"So, Zander, what exactly is a Shefir?" she asks.

My cock twitches at the sound of my name across her lips. I want to hear her say it again and again. I must be cautious with her though. "It is an honored titled bestowed upon the one who leads our tribe."

She tilts her head. "Like a chief."

"I do not know what this word *chief* means, but if it is one who the tribe follows and who makes decisions for the protection and benefit of his people, then yes, it is like that."

"So basically, you're kind of a big deal," London muses, her beautiful lips tipping up at the corners.

The sight of her smile warms me. I want to see it often and be the reason for it. Several of her words don't translate, but I can take a guess at their meaning. "Modesty prevents me from agreeing with you. About being a big deal, I mean."

Laughter bubbles out of her and she tries to smother it with a hand over her mouth. I want to capture the sound and bring it out whenever I wish. Hopefully one day, London will feel comfortable sharing all of her emotions with me.

She clears her throat and gestures over her shoulder. "I should probably go back to helping."

I step back and sweep my arm toward the door. "Of course, I don't mean to keep you."

She hesitates a fraction, but then slides past me with a quick sideways glance in my direction, the scent of lule-bore following behind her. I leave the door of the building open in case she plans on bringing more supplies inside. Falling into step beside her, we walk through the settle-ment and back toward the gates. London's eyes burn a hole in my side every time her gaze darts my way. I don't need to see it, because I can feel it.

"Are you going to follow me around all day?" she finally asks after the silence grows between us.

"I would like to offer my assistance with anything you might need."

She stops abruptly and swings to face me. "Why?"

"What do you mean?"

"I mean"—she fists her hips—"why are you offering your assistance?"

That same voice that told me she would not like me carrying things for her is also telling me not to admit that Deeka has chosen her for my mate. Not yet at least. I have no wish to frighten London. She is wary enough of me.

"Because after everything your people have been through this day, it is the right thing to do," is all I say.

Her gaze studies my face, and I keep my expression as clear and open as I can.

"Fine." She pivots and once again marches forward toward the gates.

We pass the three females that seem to be her tribe sisters. They watch us intently. The tallest one with hair the color of the fiku trees studies me with a sharp curiosity. I am glad London has them to look out for her. They have nothing to fear from me however. I will always protect my mate.

CHAPTER 6

Having a huge alien shadowing my every move is unnerving. Especially this particular alien. His heated gaze sears into me, causing an unwelcome shiver to course down my back. What does he want from me?

I unload the last of the supplies into the storage building and swipe my sweaty palms on my pant legs. Nothing about Tavikh is what we were told. Finally, I turn to Zander.

"Thank you for your help," I tell him.

He does that strange salute again and bows his head before raising just his eyes to meet mine. "It has been my pleasure."

The slight purr in his voice gives an entirely different meaning to his words, but I ignore it and the way it resonates inside me. I need to go find the girls and figure out what happens next. We step outside, the hot sun no longer overhead but hidden behind the settlement walls, and I close the door behind me. As though sensing my need for a distraction, Remi joins us.

"There you are," she says, looping her arm around mine. "Maeve and Zara are waiting for us over at the central meeting house."

I glance at Zander. "I better get going. Thanks again."

Thankfully, Remi pulls me away. Of its own accord, my head turns to peek over my shoulder. He's still standing where we left him, his bright yellow eyes locked on mine. Quickly, I turn back around and keep marching forward.

"Oh my god," she whispers loudly. "What was that all about? He kept following you around like he was going to pounce on you any minute and eat you. In a good way."

My face flames and the visual makes me shiver, because there were certainly moments I felt like Zander was going to devour me. "He was just helping me unload some of the supplies."

Remi squeezes my arm. "That was more than just helping. I mean, unless he was wanting to help you out of your clothes. His eyes undressed you every time he looked at you. Which was all the damn time."

I can't deny it, because she's right. "Apparently he's the leader of his tribe."

"Tribe? Do they live nearby?" she asks. "I wonder why they were here today. I mean, it's a good thing they were, considering those freakish monsters attacked us. That was not in the brochure, I can tell you that."

"I didn't ask him." For whatever reason, his continued presence made all thoughts leave my head and my tongue kept getting tangled. I couldn't think straight with him so close.

"I'm going to have nightmares about the Kreggies or whatever those other aliens were called. Christ on a cracker, did you see those guys?" Remi asks the clearly rhetorical question. "I thought we were going to die."

Me too. It had been terrifying.

"Anyway, besides leaving out the fact that there are evil aliens on this planet, it would seem that there's a lot those in charge of getting people to come to Tavikh didn't tell us."

I glance at her. "Like what?"

"Like the fact that this gated settlement is where everyone is living," Zara pipes up as we join her and Maeve. "We don't have our own houses, or our own plots of land. Not really. We get a tent that we can put up anywhere within the place. There's a small river just on the other side of that wall over there where we can get water for our baths, but we're responsible for filling and carrying it. They also have a community garden where we can pick out a tiny section to grow whatever we can find that will grow there."

My eyes widen with every word she says, and that feeling of dread grows larger. A stronger emotion inside me though—something like determination—rebels against it. I won't let the fear win.

I steel my spine and straighten my shoulders. "Alright, so maybe this isn't ideal, but this place—this planet—is our new home. Our new life. I refuse to let anything ruin it. We can't go back to Earth. At least I can't. I have nothing to go back to, even if I wanted to."

Silence hangs heavy between us. I shift nervously, my anxiety spiked through the roof.

"London's right," Remi says, breaking it, her gaze traveling over us. "There's nothing back there for me either. I suspect the same goes for you, Zara. Maeve too. You three are my family now. We're all each other has. We need to stick together."

She looks at me and smiles encouragingly. Just the sight of it makes the tension in my body ease. If nothing else, at least she's on my side.

"I—I'm with you guys," Maeve says quietly next to me. "You're my family too."

I reach over and squeeze her hand. We all turn to Zara.

"Oh for fuck's sake, fine." She throws up her hands, but there's a smirk on her face. "We're all one big, happy family. That doesn't mean we're going to start hugging and shit, does it?"

The four of us look at each other and then burst out laughing.

"No," I tell her, rolling my eyes. "We don't have to start hugging."

"Good." Zara nods in satisfaction. "Now, we need to figure out where we're going to sleep. I don't know about you guys, but running from killer aliens wore me out."

With that announcement, we head inside the building. The buzz of conversation grows around us. There are a few vaguely familiar faces from our time on the ship. We wander over to a line that's formed in front of a table.

"By the way," Zara says while we slowly creep forward, "your new boyfriend is hot. Even for an alien. I mean, all those muscles. And that long blond hair. Don't get me started on the tattoos he has."

For some reason, her words make my hackles rise. Which is ridiculous. Zander is an alien for god's sake. *An alien who kept looking at you like he wanted you naked beneath him.* I push away that stray thought.

"I didn't really pay much attention to him," I lie. "And he's not my boyfriend."

Remi snorts. Thankfully, the discussion is cut short as we reach the front of the line, and the two people sitting behind the table.

"Welcome to Tavikh," the woman on the right says, holding out a datapad. "Please answer all the questions so we can confirm your arrival and get you set up with your living space."

Several hours ago, people were running around screaming —dying—and there was a battle going on. Not anymore.

Everyone in here is surprisingly calm and acts as though it never happened. Or that today is just another day in their lives on Tavikh. It's a bit surreal. I take the datapad, fill in my information, and return it to her. Remi, Zara, and Maeve do the same.

"Excellent," she says and points over her shoulder. "If you'll just head to the back of the room, someone will get each of you your own tent and show you how to assemble it. You'll need to pick out where you'd like to make camp, so feel free to wander around the settlement and take a look. When you've decided, you can get set up. Then come back here and pick up your personal belongings, as well as some bedding for a sleeping pallet and several other supplies you'll need."

None of this is at all how I pictured life on Tavikh would be. I imagined a small town full of little wooden houses painted pretty colors and with small yards. I pictured planting a garden behind my house and maybe some flowers out front. Living in a tent on yellow dirt in a crowded, enclosed settlement with no running water or electricity never once crossed my mind. But I've already made a promise to myself that I'm going to make the best of it.

Everything about this place reminds me of those old days back in the Wild West my mother taught me about. It's like the books I'd been reading on the flight here. The ones I might have "borrowed" before leaving the ship and forgot to return. It's not as though anyone is going to miss them. No matter how many times I sat in the rec room and read, only a few people ever came in, and none of them bothered with the physical books. They all used the datapads.

We follow the woman's instructions and move to the back of the room to watch a tutorial given by an older gentleman, who introduces himself as Bruce, on how to set our new homes up. Once we all feel confident the tent isn't going to collapse on us in the middle of the night, he hands one to each of us and then we go outside to wander around.

Tent after tent dots the inside of the settlement, some larger than others, which I assume are for the few families that live here. There are small fire pits outside each one, but only a few are lit. There are quite a few of those purple-leaved trees within the encampment. They provide much needed shade, but that appears to be prime real estate, as most of the spots beneath them have been claimed. If we all want to stay together, then we have to find somewhere else to put down our roots.

"Do you guys have a preference of where you want to park?" I ask.

"Nowhere is jumping out at me yet," Remi says. "Personally, I'd prefer to have some place quiet and to ourselves. Although, I'm not sure how easy that's going to be."

"I'd like some place near some trees where we might get a little bit of shade," Zara adds.

"Let's keep looking. I'm sure we'll find something."

We continue walking through the settlement, our gazes traveling.

"What about there?" Maeve asks, pointing to the far corner, where half of a tree creeps over the top of the settlement wall and provides a decent bit of shadowed space. It looks pretty empty aside from two or three tents in the general area. There's definitely enough room for the four of us.

"I like it," I say. "It's close enough to the side gate near where the spring runs so we won't have to travel too far for our water. It's private. Kind of cozy. Or at least we can make it that way."

"Works for me." Remi shrugs.

"Looks like we've found our spot," Zara agrees.

With that, we set up our own tiny village, putting our tents in place near each other in a large semi-circle around the shady spot. We give ourselves enough distance between each other for a little bit of privacy.

Remi stands in the middle of the small space we've claimed with her hands on her hips. Her gaze travels to each tent. Then a huge smile breaks out on her face. "I don't know about you guys, but I like our set up."

I take in everything as well. While it's not what any of us expected when we took off from Earth, I actually think this might be better. Because we have each other. I look over at her and my grin matches hers. "It's perfect."

CHAPTER 7

Zander

Once London and her tribe sisters disappear inside the human's gathering place, I turn to go find Benham and advise him of the agreement that has taken place. As my head warrior, he knows those who would best be suited to return tomorrow and begin training. With my mate's arrival, it's even more imperative that the males here learn how to protect their people.

I pass several warriors carrying what appears to be the last of the supplies from the human's ship. Like Djale, their gazes latch onto the mating marks decorating my body and their eyes widen. At last, I discover Benham outside the settlement walls raising his voice, frustration evident in his tone, at several human males who practically cower from him.

These humans are nothing like the warriors he is used to dealing with. They seem to offend easily. Since it's best to remain on good terms with them, I draw his attention away. He sneers in disgust and walks away, leaving them to stare for only a moment before they quickly scatter, no doubt thankful to be rid of him.

Benham's gaze lands on me. Unlike the rest of our males who couldn't withhold their shock, his steps pause for only a heartbeat, and he merely blinks before continuing to close the distance between us. His expression remains blank. He's a fierce and hardened warrior with little patience for fools and even less desire for a mate.

"By Deeka's flame, please do not tell me that one of these weak humans is your Shefira?" he growls.

If it were anyone else, he would be punished for saying something so insulting about my mate. But we have known each other since we were kits. Aside from my brothers, Benham is the male I am closest to. Despite his obvious distaste for the humans, I trust him to make sure that London is always protected.

"I believe that my mate may surprise you. She and her three tribe sisters seem to possess an inner strength I have yet to witness in the males of their tribe," I remark. "However, she is also wary of me. Of our warriors. It will take time and patience to earn her trust. She will not accept me as her mate until then."

"And are you so sure she will accept you at all?" Benham asks.

I picture the way her eyes were frequently drawn to me. The way her breath would hitch just slightly the times I accidentally brushed up against her inside the storage building as she would pass me to leave. Mostly, I recall the faint scent of her arousal. It wasn't strong, but it had been present. My gaze meets Benham's.

"I have no doubt she will." Even if I have to seduce her. "But enough on that for now. I met with the two human tribe leaders. At last, they are willing to accept our help in learning how to hunt and defend their village. Pick out five males who have the patience and skills to teach the humans. Their training will begin tomorrow."

"I'll see that it is done." Benham crosses a fist over his chest.

"I must get back to our village. My brother will want to be made aware that I have found my mate. Once the human's ship has left, please gather the remaining warriors and make sure that the settlement is secure before returning."

"Yes, Shefir."

With one final glance at the gates, perhaps hoping for another glimpse of London, I turn and make my way through the field and into the forest. Beneath the fiku trees, nenaphur bushes grow and flourish. This is the time of season they bloom, with flowers whose petals are the same color as my mate's eyes.

My curiosity about her increases. Why did she leave her planet and travel to Tavikh? What are her likes? Dislikes? Her expression was often serious, as though she is a stranger to laughter. In that, we are similar. My laughter died when Zedam did. I want to learn everything about her.

I cross the invisible line marking the edge of Tavikhi territory. Our tribe has continued to prosper despite its slow growth. Kits have become increasingly more rare as fewer mated pairs have occurred. The fact that Deeka has blessed me with a mate means our village has the chance to grow again. Perhaps this is not just a test, but also a reward.

At last, I reach the clearing and village entrance. The sun has long descended, turning the forest dark, but the flames of the central fire, as well as torches outside of tents, illuminates our home and casts plenty of light. Soon, the twin moons will add their brilliance to the night sky.

"Shefir," the guard greets me.

"Rojtar. All is well?" I ask.

"Yes. The hunters have returned with more bounty, and the females have been busy preparing the evening meal in anticipation of your arrival. There have been no signs of any Krijese scouts either."

"Excellent." I enter the gates.

My feet barely disturb the dirt that covers the surface of our planet as I head toward my brother's tent. As I pass through the village, whispers greet my ears, and the prickling sensation of having many pairs of eyes dashing over me is heavy on my back. The last mate pairing of our people occurred over twenty seasons ago, so it's no wonder they're staring.

Zydon steps out of his tent and his gaze lands on me. An emotion I can't quite name flashes across his face. I approach and stop just short of him. His eyes travel over me before meeting mine.

"Your mating marks?" he says incredulously. "How? Who?"

"One of the human females, newly arrived on the latest space craft. Our warriors were at the settlement this morning just as the Krijese attacked. She and several of her tribe sisters were running to get inside the safety of the gates when she fell. I reached her first and carried her to safety. The minute my hands touched her, I felt the searing pain of them activating."

"I can't believe it. A human female is your mate?" Zydon stares in disbelief. "Does she know?"

"I did not tell her. She is wary of our presence. Based on something one of them said, I do not think that they were made aware of our existence on this planet."

My brother scoffs. "Nothing these humans do surprises me. It is no wonder they do not seem to care about what happens to the new arrivals. They haven't done anything to prepare them for what life is truly like on Tavikh."

It does seem to be the truth. London and her tribe sisters had certainly been shocked and confused by our appearance. I can only imagine how frightening the battle with the Krijese must have been for them. I do not like the fact that my mate might be scared. She should never have to fear anything. The more I learn, the more I feel bringing her to my village is the best thing to do. I don't think she will come easily though.

"I am going to return to the human settlement tomorrow and speak with her. I don't trust the males to keep her safe, despite them finally being willing to train with our warriors. I am going to try and convince her to move here." Yes, the more I think about it, the better the idea sounds.

Zydon studies me. "Are you sure that is a good idea?"

I blink. "Why would it not be?"

"You have seen what the humans are like. They do not care for us. How long have we been offering assistance—protection—and been turned away? They're as weak and defenseless as kits. They're strangers. Yet you are thinking of bringing one of their females here?" He raises his arms out.

"Of course I am. She is meant to be by my side. You don't know what it's like to have a mate," I bite out.

Zydon's expression turns stormy, and I regret my harsh tone. His lips tighten. "And you have barely had one for half a turn of the sun. One who doesn't even know she *is* your mate."

I blow out a frustrated breath. "You are right. My apologies, brother. I did not mean my insensitive words. I've never before understood the power of the mating bond though. It does not matter that London doesn't feel it yet, because *I* feel it. Deep within my soul. Even being apart from her for this short time makes my soul ache."

"I only worry about you. And our people." Zydon lays a hand on my shoulder.

That familiar unsettled sensation grows in my belly. Perhaps this is what Deeka has been trying to tell me. That I am not fit to be Shefir, because I am thinking more of my mate than my tribespeople. Maybe it is Zydon that is meant to be our leader.

"Whatever is inside that head of yours, you are wrong," he says. "You are the best one to lead our tribe. You and your Shefira. Whatever you decide, I will support you."

"Thank you, brother." I clasp his forearm and pull him to me. "Come, let us head to the central fire. Our people should be made aware that I have found my Shefira."

Zydon and I make our way toward the middle of the village. He takes a seat on one of the wooden stumps while I stand before all the tribespeople. Their curious gazes wander over the mating marks that still tingle. It's a pleasant and warm feeling, reminding me that she is so close.

"Good evening and may Deeka bless you as she has blessed me," I begin. "It would seem that my mate is among the human females that arrived today. I hope when I bring her to our village, you will welcome her with kindness."

Murmurs of, "Yes, Shefir," rise up through the village before slowly, everyone resumes what they were doing before my announcement. Talek rushes over to me and comes to an abrupt halt, staring up at me.

"Shefir, do you truly have a human mate?" he asks. "Does she look like the healer's apprentice?"

I chuckle at his curiosity. "I truly do, and no, she does not look like the healer's apprentice," No one is as beautiful as London. "They are not like the Tavikhi. Their skin and hair range in color from pale to dark like the wood from the fiku trees. Their eyes are also pale with two different colored orbs in the middle. The only similarity between her and the healer's apprentice is that they have no tail."

Talek's eyes widen even further. "But how do they travel in the trees if they have no tail to grip the branches?"

I ruffle his hair. "I do not think they climb trees."

His face wrinkles. "I do not think I would want a human mate then. Not if she could not leap and play in the trees with me."

Zydon's laughter joins mine as he approaches. "You are a wise young male. I, too, wish for a mate who likes to play in the trees."

I shoot my brother a look, but he merely peers back at me innocently. I turn my gaze back to Talek. "You are a worthy young male. I'm sure Deeka will bless you with an equally worthy female when the time is right. Now go eat something before the elders decide you are not hungry enough and give your portion to the shkaba."

"Yes, Shefir," he mumbles before running to find his nene.

Zydon snorts. "He knows none of the tribespeople would ever do that."

"Of course not, but you know as well as I that if I hadn't sent him to eat, he would have continued on about mates and climbing trees, among other questions I'm sure he would have come up with," I point out. "Curiosity is important, but eating and becoming the strong warrior I know Talek yearns to be is more important."

My brother nods. "That is why you make a good Shefir. Because you care about the needs of all our tribespeople."

"You care about them as well," I'm quick to note, because it's true.

He claps my shoulder. "I do. But you know as well as I that I'm far too impulsive and quick to action to be a good Shefir. Our people need someone who is patient and thinks things through from all the angles before making a decision. You weigh the consequences of all your actions first. That is something I do not have a talent for."

Zydon and I are certainly opposites in that regard. Zedam was more like me. "You have other talents that more than make up for it."

He smirks. "In that you speak the truth."

I shake my head. "Let us both eat before the elders decide to give *our* portions to the shkaba."

We cross to the fire and scoop out some of the leburin soup into our bowls before taking a seat on the long bench made of the fiku tree. While I sit with my meal, my gaze travels over the tribespeople gathered around talking and laughing. It's a sight that soothes my soul. I only wish that London were here with me to enjoy it.

CHAPTER 8

LONDON

With a heavy sigh, I turn to my other side, still unable to get comfortable despite trying the entire night. I've barely gotten a wink of sleep between the too-thin sleeping pallet we were given, children crying, and the occasional person passing by outside my tent. When I did manage to close my eyes, visions of a certain white-gold-haired, purple alien filled my mind. More than once I almost crept over to Remi's tent to ask if I could sleep in there with her.

The early morning sounds of people moving about clearly signal the start of the day. I groan. I'm not sure I'm going to make it through without a nap. In frustration, I toss back the fur covering and rise from the ground. I slip my feet into my shoes, finger comb my hair, and step outside.

It's just past dawn. The two moons—another thing that shocked me—are barely visible near the horizon of the settlement wall, half-hidden behind the yellow haze that seems to be a constant on the planet. The sky is filled with various colors: purples, yellows, and oranges. It's so different than the blue sky I would sometimes stare up at as I lay on the small patch of grass outside the old, abandoned library. A sky that is far, far away from here.

"Couldn't sleep?" a feminine voice asks from close by, making me jump. "That's usually how it is for the first week or so. It gets better."

I turn to locate the speaker. A young woman, perhaps a few years older than me, sits on a wooden bench in the small space between my tent and what I assume is hers. In her hands is a steaming mug.

"Sorry." She smiles sheepishly. "I didn't mean to scare you. I'm Sage, your neighbor."

"London." I glance at her tent and back to her. "Did you get here yesterday too or have you been here a while? I mean, in the settlement?"

Sage nods and takes a sip of her drink. "Six months. Give or take, anyway. Time moves a little different here than it does back on Earth. The days are slightly longer, the nights shorter."

"Yet another thing we weren't told before we left," I mumble.

She barks out a short laugh. "You have no idea."

"You're not inspiring any confidence," I joke. "But truly, at this point, I don't think anything you could tell me would surprise me. That's not a challenge though."

She scoots down the length of the narrow bench. "Have a seat if you'd like."

"Thanks." I cross the distance and lower myself next to her.

"I'd offer you something to drink, but I only have this one cup," she says.

"That's okay, thanks. So, tell me about life on Tavikh," I prod.

She gestures with a sweep of her arm. "You're looking at it. Although, yesterday was a little more excitement than we usually have. You know, with the Tavikhi and Krijese and whatnot."

Zander's face flashes behind my eyes. "Who are they? I mean, I know they're aliens who live on this planet, but where? How? And why didn't anyone tell us?"

"They're native to Tavikh and live in a village in the forest past the field out there. Every time a new ship shows up, they fight with the Krijese to try and protect us. A fact half the people here forget." Sage chuckles and takes another sip. "As for why they didn't tell anyone. Would *you* have traveled to another planet where two warring species of aliens lived if you knew ahead of time?"

My expression seems to be answer enough, because she continues, "Didn't think so."

I wince, because she's right. "Point taken. Oh, and Zander mentioned something about a translator, but I don't remember ever getting one."

Sage raises an eyebrow. "Zander, huh?"

My cheeks heat, and I ignore the insinuation in her tone. "Um, yeah, their leader. He sort of helped me yesterday."

She smirks, but doesn't push. "They inserted it during the physical exam they gave you before the trip. The needle and prick behind your ear? That was when they did it. Or so I've been told."

I vaguely recall the pinch she's referring to. A part of me feels violated by the fact that something was injected into my body without my consent. But, like Sage said, if we all knew ahead of time that we'd be cohabitating with two warring alien species, what are the chances we would have still come? Unless, of course, the only other choice was prison.

At this point, there's nothing I can do about it. We're here and this is the life we're all living—*I'm* living. My gaze wanders around the settlement again. "So, what you're saying is that we wake up every morning, sit and drink our…"

"Coffee," she supplies.

"Right, coffee, and then do nothing the rest of the day?" I ask.

"Yes and no. We're entirely self-sufficient. Which means we all have to chip in and contribute something. The nice thing is, you get to pick what you're responsible for and barter for those things you're not. For instance, if you like to sew or knit, then you get to make or repair clothes. If you like to garden, then you can grow whatever you want and buy clothes with it and vice versa."

Her words make me nervous, because I don't even know what I can contribute. I don't have any skills to note.

"Don't look so panicked." She pats my knee. "There's almost always someone available to teach you what you need to know. You only have to decide what you're remotely interested in. Take me, for example. Before I got to Tavikh, I worked as an assistant to the CEO of a biotech advancement company. I answered phones, made appointments, and fetched coffee. Here, I'm an apprentice to the Tavikhi healer and learning how to tend to wounds and any injuries."

I try to picture myself as a nurse and the image is fuzzy.

"I don't think I'd be very good at that," I admit.

Sage shoulder bumps me. "No biggie. What did you do back on Earth? Maybe there's something similar here."

My brain freezes. Panic rises up from my belly and makes my heart race. *Think, damn it.* "Um, I did a little bit of this and that. Nothing I was really any good at."

Thankfully Sage doesn't seem to notice my mini freak out. Or she's too polite to point it out. "What do you *like* to do? Even if you don't think you're good at it."

I sit for a moment, and there's only one thing I can come up with. "I love to read."

"Hmmm," she murmurs, her lips twisting to one side. Then she perks up. "What about teaching? There are quite a few kids here. Most of them school age. We don't have an official teacher or even a school, but maybe that's something you could start?"

At first I want to tell her I'm no teacher, but then the idea grabs hold. Could I actually do it? Would the parents even *want* me to? The more it rattles around inside my head, the more my excitement grows. I try to temper it, because prior experience has made me leery of hoping for too much.

"Do you really think so?" I can't help but ask. "I mean, I'm not really qualified to teach. And the only subject I am good at is reading and maybe a little bit of history."

"Maybe you could get together with one of the Tavikhi tribe members and learn about Tavikh's history. Teach the kids about previous life here. This *is* the planet they're going to grow up on after all," Sage suggests. "You're welcome to come with me tomorrow when I go to the village. Meet with some of the elders there."

An instant refusal comes to my lips, and I open my mouth to tell her so, but we're interrupted by Remi.

"Good morning," she says, coming to stand by us. Her gaze lands on my new friend, and she smiles in greeting. "Hi, I'm Remi."

"Sage."

"We were just talking about jobs and what we might be able to do here. It seems like everything works on a barter system," I explain.

"What do you mean?" Remi starts to lower herself to the ground, but pauses part way. "Wait, we should probably get Zara and Maeve so you only have to explain it once."

"We're already here," Zara says from behind her.

The three of us turn and find Maeve and her approaching.

"Oh good," I say. "Guys, this is Sage. She's our neighbor and was just telling me about how the settlement is run."

For a second time, she walks us through things. Assigned tasks. Bartering. Everything about what our new life is going to be like.

"She thinks I could teach the village kids," I tell my friends once Sage finishes. "It's honestly the only thing I think I would be good at. What about you guys? What would you want to do?"

"Hell if I know," Zara scoffs from her seated position on the ground she and the others took. "I want to know what my options are, I guess. Like what is something that really needs to be done?"

Everyone turns to Sage. She's the one who's been here the longest and knows more than we do.

"I'm not sure." She nibbles her lip. "I did hear about one thing, but I doubt it would be something any of you are interested in."

Remi tips her head and a skeptical expression crosses her face. "Like what?"

Sage hesitates and doesn't meet anyone's gaze.

"Spit it out," Zara demands.

"Fine." She huffs. "Apparently, the rumor around the settlement is that the Tavikhi are returning today to train the men on how to fight and hunt. It's possible they may be willing to train the women as well, if anyone wanted to, that is."

My heart leaps in my chest. They're coming back? Today? Does that mean Zander will be here? *Why do I even care*?

"I'm in," Remi proclaims.

My jaw drops. "What? What do you mean you're in?"

Her expression turns fierce. "All my life, I was told what to wear. How to act. 'Don't do this, Remington.' 'Don't do that, Remington.' I escaped to a whole new planet for a reason. Finally, I'm free to do anything I want. There's no one to criticize me. To nitpick. I can be someone who isn't slowly being suffocated to death."

We all stare at her in shock. None of us had any idea. How could we? We've all held our secrets close.

"Remington? Your name is *Remington*?" Zara snickers. "Jesus, no wonder you ran away."

I press my lips together and glance at Maeve and Sage, who both appear to be trying to smother their own smiles. Remi glares at her. "*That* is what you got from me spilling my guts? You're going to make fun of my name?"

Zara nods manically. "Um, yeah. Who the fuck names their kid—their *daughter*—Remington anyway? Sounds like you're better off without those people. I know I'm better off without my shit parents as well."

"I am too," Sage adds.

A part of me wants to snap at them. At least they have parents. But maybe having terrible parents is worse. At least I always knew I was loved.

"My mother is dead," I say quietly. "And I'd give anything to be able to spend even one more minute with her."

"So is mine," Maeve adds just as softly.

"Ah, damn it." Zara wraps her in a gentle hug. "I'm sorry, Mae. You too, London. That was an asshole thing for me to say."

We all sit quietly for a minute, silently coming to terms with our losses, until finally, Remi clears her throat. "Back to our previous discussion. I'm joining the men and training with the Tavikhi. I want to experience everything our new home has to offer. And I want to contribute in some way that matters for me. So I guess that just leaves Zara and Maeve to decide what they want."

"I think I'd be good at gardening," Maeve says with a fair amount of confidence. "Maybe I can grow some flowers or, better yet, some fruits or vegetables. I'll just need to figure out what might flourish in the soil here."

I love how the excitement seems to be growing in all of us. Then we turn to Zara, who simply shrugs.

"I have no idea, but I'm sure I'll figure something out soon," she says. "Which is probably good, because it looks like our friendly alien neighbors just showed up."

We all turn in the direction she's pointing. Sure enough, the gates have been opened, and with the pale sun just cresting the horizon, a small group of Tavikhi warriors stride through with their tails lashing behind them, power evident in every step they take. And leading them is Zander.

CHAPTER 9

ZANDER

Anticipation thrums through my veins with the knowledge that London is nearby. My sleep had been restless. My furs feeling more empty than ever. As our warriors and I stride toward the central meeting place, my gaze travels through the settlement, bouncing from tent to tent as I search for my mate. The faces of the humans wandering around express curiosity, caution, and outright distrust.

The sensation of eyes on me draws my gaze to the back corner. Standing with her three tribe sisters, as well as a fourth female I recognize as Kyler's apprentice, is London. She watches me with a mix of emotions, but the one I latch onto is the one that makes her breath catch. Even with the distance that separates us, it is noticeable in the parting of her lips and the flash in her gaze. Tension crackles between us, igniting tiny sparks along my mating marks that burn with pleasure-pain.

With a raised hand, my warriors stop outside the human's gathering place, but I continue moving forward, drawn to the slight scent of arousal from my mate which floats on the wind. I don't stop until I'm close enough to reach out and touch her. I resist the temptation, but only barely.

"Good morning, London." My voice is almost a husky growl.

She stares up at me and then shakes her head, blinking, as though breaking free of a mystical spell placed upon her by Deeka.

"Morning," she replies, her cheeks turning the color of manerrat berries.

"Did you sleep well?"

"Fine, thank you."

I nod but am unable to resist a confession. "I am glad for it. Although, I will admit I did not, but only because all my waking thoughts were filled with you, and I didn't want to risk closing my eyes and having you disappear."

London's eyes widen and her mouth drops open, although she quickly recovers. "You can't say something like that to me."

I stare at her in confusion. "Why not?"

"Be—be—because," she sputters. "You just don't say something like that to a person."

"It is only the truth I speak." London can deny it all she wants, but there is something between us. Something that draws us together. It is fate and Deeka's will.

"Okay, Romeo, let's bring the intensity down just a fraction," one of her tribe sisters says.

I glance at her in surprise. It is the small one with hair similar in color to the Tavikhi. I've been so focused on my mate that I forgot we had company. "Romeo? I do not know who you speak of. My name is Zander," I remind her.

She barks out a laugh. "Never mind. What I'm saying, buddy, is that you need to lay off the smooth talk just a little, okay?"

Once again, several of her words don't translate, but it would seem as though my declaration has unsettled my mate. Frustration builds, but I push it down. I must learn to be patient. "As you wish. I merely wanted to wish London a good morning. And a good morning to her tribe sisters."

The four of them offer their own greeting. It is apparent that if I am to win over my mate, I must also earn the trust of these human females. I turn back to London. "I will take my leave of you while I meet with the tribe leaders so training can begin."

I cross my fist over my chest and turn away to head over to where my warriors—and the two human leaders—stand outside of the gathering building. The heat of my mate's gaze on me remains.

"Are your males ready?" I ask the moment I reach them.

The elder of the two nods. "They are. At least the ones who are able. We have some children and a few elderly who aren't able to join us."

"Our kits learn how to hunt just as our warriors do," I tell them.

"Well, human children are different," he insists.

Instead of pushing the issue, I merely nod. There is no point in arguing with them. I am not the leader of their people. Slowly, the males approach. It's clear that at least half of them aren't happy with our presence. The rest seem cautious, with only a few eager faces present. I introduce the five warriors Benham chose to train the humans, and soon they head outside the settlement to begin.

I turn and come face to face with one of London's tribe sisters. The one with hair the color of the fiku tree and who seems the most protective of my mate.

"Zander, right?" she asks, boldly meeting my gaze.

I dip my head in respect. "How may I be of service?"

"I'll be joining your warriors for training." There's no hesitancy in her statement. Her shoulders are straight, and she holds her head up high as though daring me to contradict her.

"What is your name, female?"

"Remi," she says and almost stands even taller.

I study her critically, taking in everything about her. She returns my gaze without flinching. She's taller than London and more slender, but compared to even the females in my village, she is small. Certainly no match for any Tavikhi warrior or Krijese. However, she seems to possess confidence and determination.

"What makes you think I should allow this?"

Her expression tightens and her fists clench at her side. She tilts her chin up and fire spits from her eyes. "I wasn't asking your permission."

I admire her spirit. No doubt she will make a fearsome warrior, despite being female. "Perhaps it is not my permission you need to seek. However, my warriors answer to me, and they follow my orders."

Remi opens her mouth, but I hold up a hand. "Becoming a fighter is a difficult task. My warriors will not take it easy on you just because you are female. Are you sure that this is something you are fully prepared for?"

"I didn't ask for you to make it easy on me," she grinds out. "In fact, I'll actually be pissed if you do."

A laugh nearly spills from my lips, but I manage to withhold it. Oh yes, London's tribe sister is a fierce one. She will make a fine mate for someone. That gives me pause. Will any of these other humans trigger another warrior's mating marks? If Deeka saw fit to grant me a human mate, will there be others in my tribe that she will grant the same?

"My warriors will be here before the sun rises each morning. You will meet with them and train," I finally tell Remi.

Her fists unclench and the tightness in her shoulders releases. "Thank you."

I dip my head and she returns the gesture before walking back to where the rest of her tribe sisters, including London, wait with a nervous energy I can feel from here. It's evident in their restless movements. She reaches them and begins speaking. Their expressions shift to surprise, with several glances in my direction. I can only assume they didn't think I would so easily say yes to Remi's demand. Moments later, she leaves the group and rushes across the settlement and out the gate where the warriors and human males disappeared.

It is as I told Benham. There is a hidden strength within these human females. I believe they could make a worthy mate to any of my tribe brothers. With the males gone, the rest of the humans return to their tasks. I observe them. There is a strange sort of chaos to their movements. Their village runs nothing like ours. They don't work as a unit for the benefit of everyone. It's as though each one is focused only on themselves or their singular family instead of the settlement as a whole.

Which means that no one is taking care of London, except perhaps her tribe sisters. I head in their direction. My need to make sure that my mate is taken care of is strong. This is the perfect time to try and convince her to come to my village instead. She'll be protected and want for nothing.

I only have eyes for her, but I sense the gaze of the other females as I reach their small circle again. "Perhaps you can show me around your village?"

She blinks and glances at her tribe sisters and back to me. "There's not really much to see. I mean, you were just here yesterday."

"This is true. But I saw the village through my own eyes. I would like to see it through yours," I tell her. "I also would like to discuss something with you."

"With me?" London asks, drawing back. "What would you need to talk to me about?"

"Let us walk, yes?" I'd rather not have an audience. Plus, I would like to spend more time alone with my mate. Yesterday was not nearly enough.

Her sisters wave her on, almost encouraging her to join me. She hesitates briefly before taking several steps forward, and then falls in line next to me. As we travel through the settlement, London is quiet. I sense unease from her, although I'm not sure if it has anything to do with me specifically. I have no wish for her to be unsettled around me. "Is our planet very different from Earth?"

She glances over at me and laughs softly. "You have no idea."

"How so?"

"Well, let's see. We only have one moon. Half the planet is covered in water. Our sky is blue, and our grass is green. Same with the leaves on the trees. Dirt is brown, not yellow. We live in tall buildings that feel like they could touch the clouds, not in tents barely big enough for a sleeping pallet. We have indoor plumbing." She holds up a finger for each difference she rattles off. "The list goes on. Oh, and we don't have vicious aliens trying to kill us."

I'm fascinated by all of these things, even if I can't picture any of it. There's also a note of longing in her tone. "It sounds like you miss it? Which makes me wonder what brought you here."

I admit to being glad for it though. There is a reason Deeka chose London as my mate. She sighs at my side. "There was nothing left for me back on Earth."

My gaze flicks to her. The longing seems to have turned to pain. My mating marks burn with the need to soothe her. "I am sorry for that. But I am also glad you are here."

She stops in the middle of the village and stares at me. "I don't understand you or what you seem to want from me."

"I want to make sure you are protected. It's not safe in the settlement," I tell her. "I think it would be best if you came to my village to stay."

London's eyes widen. "Why?"

Unable to resist the temptation any longer, I close the distance between us. Her head tips back as she stares up at me. Desire flickers in her eyes and the scent of her arousal grows stronger. I palm her cheek, the skin soft beneath mine, and my clawed fingers tunnel through her hair. I take great care not to scratch her. My tail rises and wraps around her waist to pull her even closer. London's hands go to my chest as though to brace herself. She sucks in a sharp breath and freezes.

"Because you are my *keeshla*. My fated mate."

CHAPTER 10

Fated mate? *Keeshla*?

Already, I'm shaking my head. There's no such thing.

"My mating marks prove otherwise," Zander says softly and takes a tiny step back, his hand dropping from my face. I find myself leaning the slightest bit forward as though trying to recapture his touch.

I blink as his words register. Had I said that out loud? It doesn't matter, because it's true. Fated mates don't exist. "What do you mean, mating marks? Is that what those tattoos are?"

He glances down at his body and my gaze follows, almost leisurely traveling over not only the dark markings, but the sculpted chest and chiseled abs before dropping a little more southerly. The already impressive bulge beneath his pants gets even bigger. I jerk my eyes back up to meet his. The heat in his expression sears me to the bone. His yellow eyes darken like he can read the carnal thoughts running through my mind, although considering where my gaze had lingered, it's no surprise.

"All male Tavikhi are born with marks on their skin. The moment we meet our fated mate, they burn and darken in color. My marks were triggered when I touched you yesterday. Our goddess, Deeka, blessed me with you for a mate," Zander says with no small amount of awe in his voice. It washes over me and settles like a warm blanket. It's a pleasant, comforting sensation I haven't felt since before my mother died. It can't be though.

"Even if I believed in fated mates,"—I hold up my hand when it appears like he's going to interrupt me—"I can't just up and leave the settlement and go to your village."

His ridged brow creases. "But you are my mate. I can protect you much better than the males here can. I will also be able to provide you with anything you'll need."

There's a small part of me that actually wants to take Zander up on his offer. Not because of this fated mate business, but because just knowing that the Krijese could attack again at any moment makes my heart race and a lump form in my belly. It would also be nice to have someone take care of me for once. My mother had done her best, but she'd always struggled. After she got sick, I was the one who had to learn to take care of everything.

"I can't. This is my new home, such that it is. I won't abandon it, or my friends, just because it might be easier,"

I tell him firmly.

Once again Zander's tail wraps around me, and he tugs me against him. His woodsy scent almost makes me dizzy with desire. I have to resist him though. He leans down until his thick, luscious lips nearly touch my ear. His hot and surprisingly sweet-smelling breath tickles my skin and sends a shiver coursing down my back. I tilt my head, unconsciously giving him better access.

"I have never been one to back down from a challenge, *keeshla*," he whispers. "I will find a way to convince you that we are fated to be together."

Zander nips at my ear. My knees are weak, and I would have melted into a puddle on the hard, yellow ground if not for his tail holding me up. Moments pass before I finally feel steady. Only then does he loosen his hold. I shouldn't let him affect me and yet he does. The fire in his eyes tells me we both know it. Before I can work up the indignation to disagree with him, he turns and walks away, leaving me standing in the middle of the village, staring after him.

I raise my hand to my chest to try and calm my racing heart. My feet keep me frozen until Zander strides through the front gate and disappears from view. It's only then I become aware of the stares from everyone around me. My cheeks flush and I hurry back to my tent and my waiting friends.

Zara is the first to pipe up. "What the hell was that all about? I thought he was going to kiss you right then and there."

Unable to speak yet, I drop onto the bench between my tent and Sage's. Maeve comes and sits next to me. Her hand grips mine in a comforting gesture. It snaps me out of the haze of arousal Zander left me in. I send her a grateful smile and then breathe deeply before glancing at Zara and Sage. "He seems to think I'm his fated mate sent here by his goddess. Those dark purple tattoos are apparently his mating marks. They only turn that color when he's met his…*keeshla* I think he called it. And he wants me to move to his village with him so he can supposedly protect and care for me."

"Are you shitting me?" Zara blurts out far too loudly.

Still slightly dazed, I just nod.

"There are worst things that could happen, I guess," she says.

My head jerks up and I stare at her. "Like what?"

She lifts a single shoulder. "You have a sexy alien telling you you're his mate. You could be living in luxury and getting waited on hand and foot. Not to mention the fact that a *hot, sexy alien* obviously wants to do the dirty with you. From where I'm standing, that's a pretty sweet deal."

My jaw drops and I nearly choke on my spit. The idea is so ludicrous, I can't help but laugh. "Only you would think it was a good idea."

Zara flashes her signature smile, the one that always manages to appear mischievous. It quickly disappears and she moves to sit on the ground at my feet. She looks up at me with a far more serious expression than she usually wears. "I'm not saying you should immediately take him up on the offer, but I'm also not saying you should say no without thinking it over. Not just for the alien dick either."

I snort, because once again, Zara is being Zara. "Regardless, you guys are my family, and I have no intention of abandoning you to go off to some alien village with, as you say, 'a hot sexy alien'."

"Pfft, as if we'd let you abandon us anyway," Maeve says with a shocking strength. I squeeze her hand and shoulder bump her.

"You're not going to get rid of me that easily." And yet, now that the thought has been planted, I can't seem to not think about it.

"Well since that seems to be settled," Sage pipes up. "We should probably get our day started. There's a lot to get done."

We all nod. She isn't wrong. Zara still hasn't decided what she's going to do, and Maeve and I need to find whoever's in charge of the job list so we can notify them of our plans. I glance toward the front gate. "I wonder how Remi is doing with the men."

"I'm sure she's holding her own. You know how she is," Zara says.

It's true. There's a fire burning inside our friend to do whatever it is she can, and no one is going to tell her otherwise. It's a trait I wish I possessed. But the fear that's always lived inside me won't loosen its hold. Although maybe being here, on Tavikh, is the first step. Zander's voice whispers in my ear. Fated mates? It can't be. Yet there's no denying there's something about him that keeps drawing me in.

Enough.

"Alright, come on, Maeve. Let's go find…" I glance at Sage expectantly.

"Alice," she supplies. "She would have been one of the women who checked you in yesterday. Older woman with short brown hair and glasses."

"Right, Alice. Hopefully they're open to our interests." I tug Maeve up off the bench and we head toward the central meeting building. That seems to be where the welcoming committee tends to hang out.

Sure enough, the same woman who sat behind the table yesterday is in the building sorting through the remaining supplies and appearing to be taking inventory.

"Hi, are you Alice?" I ask.

She turns to us with a pleasant smile. "That's me. What can I do for you?"

"We understand you're the one we speak to about how we've chosen to contribute to the settlement."

"Yes, have you decided what you'd like to be in charge of then?" she asks.

I share a glance with Maeve and gather my courage. "From my understanding, there's no formal schooling here. I'd like to offer teaching services to the children. I have a few books in print, and you guys have some datapads, which will help them to read and write. I also know a lot about history. Admittedly, math isn't my best subject, but I have some rudimentary skills. Enough to teach the younger ones how to add and subtract at least."

"Hmmm," Alice murmurs and turns to Maeve. "What about you?"

My friend clears her throat nervously but takes what I'd call a fortifying breath and straightens. "I'm interested in agriculture. Growing food or herbs. Anything that will take to the ground here."

"I'll have to run your suggestions by the council leaders, Gary and Adam, but I don't think either one of them will be a problem. I'm sure the parents will be grateful for a break, and with the settlement expanding, there's always need for more food," Alice says.

That little flame of hope that had nearly extinguished, flares to life. I've been so conditioned to things not going my way, even the hint of possibility is enough for excitement to bloom. "Thank you so much. We really appreciate it."

"Of course. As soon as I see them, I'll bring it up," she tells us. "Stop back by later this afternoon and I should have an answer for you."

I nod. "Thanks again."

Maeve and I wave goodbye and head back outside. She nudges my arm. "That sounded promising."

"It did. You didn't think I came across as too desperate or unqualified, do you?" I worry my bottom lip.

"Not at all. You told her what you could bring to it but were also honest about what isn't your strong suit. I think that works in your favor. They know you're truthful and not just trying to sell them on knowledge you don't actually have. I think that would be worse."

I wobble my head slightly side to side. "Yeah, you're probably right."

We make it back to where Zara and Sage have gotten a couple fires going in front of our tents and what appears to be breakfast cooking.

"How'd it go?" Zara asks, poking at the brown lump sizzling on a skillet over the flames.

"Alice has to run it by the council leaders first, but she's pretty sure we'll be given the go-ahead," I tell her.

Sage nods as she pours two mugs of steaming hot coffee and passes them to Maeve and me. "Yeah, that's pretty standard."

The four of us sit down around the fires. I'm content for the moment, sitting in the quiet with friends I never expected to have while I stare out over the settlement and observe people going about their daily tasks. Several children dart around, and I count them in my head, as well as assessing about how old they are. I've never really been around kids, but I'm sure it will be fine. Being a teacher shouldn't be that hard.

CHAPTER 11

Zander

Such a stubborn female my London is turning out to be. I shouldn't be surprised by her insistence to remain with her tribe sisters. Still, I can't control the helpless sensation that fills me. It's not often I feel like this. The last time was when Zedam went missing.

I stand just outside the settlement gates and observe the training going on. The human males are sloppy and undisciplined. It's no wonder their hunts often end in disappointment. How did they survive back on their planet? Did they not have to gather their own food or protect their families? It makes me curious as to what their leaders back on Earth told them about Tavikh that they don't have any life skills.

My gaze wanders until it lands on London's tribe sister. Fatigue is evident on her face and body, but there's also a marked determination about her that reminds me of our youngest warriors, desperate to prove themselves. Her technique is better than most of the human males, but her lack of comparative strength is clear. Djale knocks the wooden staff out of her hand, but she quickly picks it up and faces off against him again.

Benham comes striding toward me. Irritation radiates from him. He stops at my side and turns his gaze to the practice. I've learned it is best to wait for him to speak when he has something to say.

"They are worse than the kits," he finally says with a snarl of disgust after a few moments of silence.

"Which is why they are training. Even young Talek is still learning. At least they appear to be trying."

He grunts, but there is a begrudging hint of approval behind it. "I am surprised you allowed the female to join."

"She is one of my *keeshla's* tribe sisters. There is a certain inner strength to her that I did not want to crush. Besides, the female made it more than clear that she was going to train whether I granted permission or not." I nearly smile at the memory of her fierce declaration.

Benham glances over at me. "Still, do you think it wise?"

I clap him on the shoulder. "If I am going to win my *keeshla*, I am going to need all the allies I can get. She is strong in mind, if not quite in body yet. My guess is she will do just as well as, if not better than, some of the males. And the humans need as many people protecting them as they can get."

"If she is going to fight, she will need a weapon that fits her smaller hands and does not carry the weight our swords do," he remarks. "Although she wields the stick well."

I'm barely able to conceal my surprise at Benham's words. He only offers praise of those truly deserving. "I trust you will make her something appropriate?"

He jerks his head sharply. "I will begin on it when I return to the village."

"You have my thanks." I rise to leave, needing to join our other warriors on the hunt. "Have them train until the sun is halfway to its zenith. Remind them we will return in the morning."

"Yes, Shefir."

Trusting Benham to take care of things, I cross the field and disappear into the forest. My steps are light amid the blades of grass while I scan the surroundings. The silence around me is soothing and gives me time to think of London back at the settlement. The way her eyes flared with attraction at my nearness. Regardless of what she says, there is an awareness between us. A spark. I only need to discover what will cause it to burn brighter.

To my right, a branch snaps. I reach for the sword at my hip just as a Krijese, with his own weapon drawn, steps out from behind a tree. With a roar, he rushes me, slashing out with the long, wooden-handled blade. I sidestep and raise both arms, blocking the strike. Sparks fly from metal against metal. We dance around each other before he charges once more. Blow after blow, we fight. What he lacks in speed, he makes up for in strength. I stumble back with the next jarring hit, but quickly recover as he moves to strike.

I spin to the left and my sword slices along his thigh, drawing blood that runs down his leg. Still, the deadly sharp edge of his weapon catches me. A small, stinging cut lines my arm, but I ignore the slight pain. He attempts to dodge my next swing, but his injury makes him uncoordinated, giving me the opening I need to drive the tip of my sword through his neck. His mouth slit peels open, and a gurgle rumbles up from his throat only to choke off completely when I shove the blade even farther into his body.

He drops his weapon to the forest floor, and it hits with a dull thud. I pull my sword from him and, for several beats, he remains unsteady on his feet, until, at last, he collapses as well. Green blood pools beneath him. I suck in ragged breaths as my gaze scans the surrounding forest for any more hidden enemies. When the air around me remains still and no shouts of rage come, I slowly relax my stance.

What was this lone Krijese up to on this side of the human settlement? He is far from his people. The only conclusion I can come to is he was a scout trying to find ways to sneak into our village. I stare down at him a moment longer before taking off toward the hunting grounds and leaving him there for the shkaba to scavenge. Remaining extra alert, I run through the trees, leaping over fallen logs, until, at last, I reach the clearing at the edge of our territory. There, I slow, confident that whichever warrior is keeping watch will warn me of any approaching danger.

I cut through another small section of fiku trees, and the call of a mellenje reaches me. There is a slight pause and another one sounds from a short distance away. I return the signal, and two hunters step out from behind the shadows.

"Shefir," Evren greets me with a fist over his chest.

"How goes the hunt?"

"I believe we have found a luani cave. We were just about to return to the village for assistance when you approached," he says.

My heart pumps at the news. It has become more difficult over the last few seasons to locate the vicious beasts with teeth nearly as long as my arm and jagged claws that can easily bring a warrior down with a single swipe. It takes several males to defeat one. But their hides make for excellent coverings during the cold season, and their meat is some of the most tender.

"Let us go and take down one of the mighty beasts then, so we can celebrate our success tonight."

Cheers from our tribespeople ring out as we pull the carcass of the luani behind us. None of us came away from our battle unscathed, but thankfully our injuries are only minor.

"See to your wound," I instruct Evren, whose broken and bloodied arm dangles at his side.

He nods and heads in the direction of the healer's tent, a grimace of pain flashing across his face, passing Zydon on his way.

"A successful hunt, I see," my brother says, his gaze focused behind me. "It has been many moon's passing since anyone has spotted a luani."

I glance back to find several warriors taking charge of moving the beast. The females will attend to stripping everything useful from it. "They are becoming far more rare as the Krijese encroach on our hunting lands. Soon there will be none left."

The two of us walk toward my tent so I can clean the blood from myself and tend to the minor wounds I received.

"Did you speak with your female?" Zydon asks with a pointed stare.

"She refused to come to the village," I admit. "For the moment, at least."

We reach my dwelling and I lift the hide to step inside. Embers glow from the central fire. I move to stoke it, but my brother waves me off. "I will attend to this. Clean your wounds. I have no desire for you to die from the blood disease."

With a slight snort, I step to the low table and basin of water. Gently, I wash away the signs of battle. Once I finish, I reach into one of the many trunks for the healing salve. I dip my finger in and spread it over each cut. By tomorrow, they should all be nearly healed. Once I have put the jar away, I turn to Zydon.

"On my way back from my visit, before I joined the hunters, I was attacked by a lone Krijese within the forest walls not far from the human settlement."

His head jerks up and he pauses poking at the rising flames. "What was he doing there? Are you certain he was alone?"

"There did not appear to be another with him, unless they remained hidden and watching. I can only assume he was some type of scout, looking for weaknesses in our border security."

Zydon's expression twists in rage. "They are growing increasingly bolder about encroaching on our territory. Unless we do something, they will not stop."

My brother is correct. On more than one occasion our baba attempted to gain some sort of truce between our tribes. The former Krijese leader was never willing to negotiate. His son, Armik, who took over leadership several moons ago, is no different. All they know is greed and war.

"Then we will continue to send their warriors to the land of their gods," I vow.

Nothing, and no *one*, will harm my mate or our people.

CHAPTER 12

The bright yellow moons are just rising in the lavender sky. The scent of burning wood from our own personal central fire makes me need to sneeze. It's an interesting fragrance of something sweet like fruit, but mixed with a lighter, more pungent odor. The five of us sit in a half-circle around it on logs Maeve and I brought in earlier today. While the Tavikhi were still present, we ventured outside the settlement wall and gathered the logs and hauled in buckets of water for washing and cooking. Afterward, we organized all our supplies and made lists of anything we thought we might need. Sage and I cooked our afternoon and evening meals. I can't remember a day where I've been this exhausted.

"I'm going to sleep like the dead tonight. Because that's exactly how I feel." With an arm slung over her face, Remi lies on the ground next to her and Maeve's log on a blanket she dragged out of her tent. The whites of the bandages wrapped around her hands glow brightly in the darkened night. Sage had applied some type of healing salve to help the blisters she'd earned while training.

"Are we regretting our decision to become a warrior queen?" Zara asks in a sing-song tone, a hint of amusement underscoring it.

Remi groans and sits up to glare at our smirking friend. "At least London, Maeve, and I have found our way of contributing to the settlement. I don't see you stepping up and doing anything."

The corner of Zara's mouth flattens and she glances away, while the rest of us shift uncomfortably in the tense silence that's fallen. I clear my throat with the sudden need to keep the peace between us. I've never had friends before. I don't want to lose any of the ones I've made. "I think we're all really tired after a long day. Let's get a goodnight sleep, and we'll feel better in the morning."

Maeve and I start to rise, but Zara's voice makes us pause. "Remi's right."

Maeve, Remi, and I share a glance and we sit back down. The heavy awkwardness returns while we wait for her to continue. Zara stares into the fire, the glow causing an eerie light to dance across her face. Just when the silence stretches long enough that maybe she won't say anything else, she does.

"I haven't found a way to contribute because I can't *do* anything. I've never had to." She pauses and takes a deep breath. "My whole life, everything has been done for me. Someone cleaned my room. Served me my meals. Picked out my clothes. Even dressed me for fuck's sake. The only thing I've ever done for myself disgraced my parents and got me kicked off Earth. I'm not athletic like Remi or well-read like London. All I know how to do is let other people take care of me. And I'm scared I'll fuck something up and let you guys down. Just like I did my parents."

I'm frozen with disbelief. Not once would I have expected that to be Zara's story. She's always so confident and self-assured. A shuffling noise makes me turn. Remi is slowly standing from the ground. She walks around the edge of the fire to where Zara sits and stands over her. Zara tips her head back. And then Remi gets down on her knees and reaches out for Zara's hand.

There's a little nudge inside me and I move to sit on the log next to Zara, our shoulders touching. Maeve joins us seconds later, settling on her other side and sitting as close to her as I am. Even Sage comes over to complete our small circle. Beside me, Zara sniffles.

"We're not the same people we were back home. The minute we boarded that spaceship, our new lives started. Nothing from our past matters. We're sitting here, on another planet in another galaxy, with a clean slate. And, yes, it's fucking scary. But we have each other now. You're not going to fuck anything up or let us down so long as you try." Remi tightens her grip on Zara's hand. "I grew up in the same type of home as you, so I understand the smothering. My parents would die if they saw me. Remington Alcott wouldn't try and learn how to become a warrior or hunter. She wouldn't dare pick up a weapon and try to wield it. But Remi would. If only to prove something to herself. Do you think I know what the hell I'm doing? I'm going to learn though. And you will too."

There's a brief pause before Zara throws her arms around Remi and chokes out a thank you through her tears. I rub her back, trying to offer my support. Every word Remi spoke echoes in my head. I'm also not the same person I was back on Earth. Which means I won't let my past define my future. Finally, Remi and Zara break apart. They both swipe away the tears tracking their cheeks.

Without another word, we all get up and start breaking down our mini campfire to get ready for bed. Sage dumps dirt over the flames, while Maeve and I separate the bowls and utensils we'd set out to dry after dinner. Remi tries to pick up her blanket with her bandaged hands, but Zara waves her away and does her best to shake off the yellowed dirt and fold it before handing it to her. It's a messy job, but she did her best.

Just before Sage enters her tent, I walk toward her. The other three disappear inside their own.

"Can I talk to you for a second?" I ask her.

"Sure, what's up?"

"If the offer's still open, I'd like to go to the Tavikhi village with you the next time. Maybe you were right about learning this planet's history and the ways of its people if I'm going to be teaching." Maeve and I checked back in with Alice and she'd given us both the go-ahead. I was so excited but also nervous.

Sage blinks and jerks slightly like I've surprised her. "Of course it's still open. I'm going in the morning."

I nod. "Okay, thanks. I guess I'll see you then."

With a small wave, I turn around and head back to my tent. I open the flap and let it slap shut behind me. A soft glow from the lantern gives off just enough light to make the interior visible so I don't stumble over everything. After changing into my sleep clothes, I carefully fold up my discarded outfit and set it on the low table for washing tomorrow. I crawl into my bedding and stare up at the rounded ceiling. My thoughts slowly drift to Zander.

Is it truly possible that a thing such as fated mates exists? He believes so. I'm not sure I do though. It doesn't seem real that a mysterious entity out in the ether somewhere decides that two people are destined for each other. *And yet, you're here. On this planet, far from Earth, where aliens live. Including one who says you're his mate.* Is there any harm in at least getting to know him? It doesn't have to lead to anything.

It doesn't matter that he's the first man to make me take notice. It's not even his muscular body and oddly handsome face despite the clear differences that mark him as not human, although those certainly are both bonuses. Really though, it's the way he so obviously wanted to help me carry all the boxes I carted into the settlement the day we arrived but gave me the room to do things for myself. The fact that I could have been killed if not for him. The way that, even deep down inside where I don't want to admit it, he makes me feel safe. Protected.

A part of me has to admit I'm going with Sage tomorrow because I'm curious. What are his people like? How many of them are there? The warriors he brought with him today all seem to respect him. Does he have family? What would it be like to live there? It's clear we don't have what it takes to fight the bad guys on our own. I shudder with the memory of the terrifying appearance of the Krijese and how brutal they were. I push it out of my mind and turn onto my side, tucking my hands beneath my cheeks. No sense in borrowing trouble.

My eyes grow heavy and burn from tiredness. I close them and breathe deeply in and out, trying to release my worries and tension. I'm floating in that stage between waking and sleeping when a sharp cry jolts me fully awake. Another shout joins the first, and then more until deep, bellowing roars add to the noise. I jump up and fling open the flap of my tent. One by one, all my friends exit theirs. We rush to each other and glance around the darkness.

Black shadows rush around, faintly illuminated by the burning fires scattered around. The screams grow louder.

"What's going on?" I ask.

"Oh god." Sage points. "The Krijese are attacking. We need to run."

Run? Run where? We're inside the settlement walls. The putrid scent of something burning reaches me and I nearly gag. Remi grabs me.

"C'mon, we have to go," she growls harshly, her practice staff in her hand.

We take off toward the perimeter wall. I glance behind me. Maeve's pale and terror-stricken, but she's right behind me. Zara and Sage trail her. We reach the wooden barrier and rush along it, trying to stay within the darkened areas where no firelight can reach us. Chaos reigns. Krijese and humans alike are running around. Some of the men are trying to fight off the grotesque aliens, but they're being taken down one by one.

My breath sounds harsh in my ears. At last, we reach the side door that leads to the river. A far too-close scream ricochets inside my head. I turn and yell at the sight before me. One of the Krijese has Sage bound against his chest. She's kicking and screaming, trying to get loose. Remi runs past me and swings her staff. It crashes against the alien's head with a loud crack. He releases Sage and she drops to the ground in a puddle. Zara drags her to her feet. Remi hits the guy again, this time bashing in his knee. Her expression is murderous.

I rush over and grab her arm. "We have to go."

It takes a couple of tugs, but finally she turns to me. There's a wild light in her eyes, but she blinks and it's gone. As though coming out of some stupor, she nods, and once again, we're at the door, although this time, Sage and Zara have managed to open it. We slip out through the gate and close it behind us. A sharp whistle comes from a short distance away. There, at the edge of the river, is a Tavikhi warrior.

"Come, Shefira, we have to get you and your tribe sisters to safety," he says, his gaze locked on mine.

Not questioning the name, we follow him, splashing through the water and reaching the other side. I glance back toward the home I'd only had for two days. Flames rise over the settlement walls. Screams and roars continue inside. I'm torn. I don't want to leave people behind, but I also don't want to die.

The Tavikhi warrior pats my arm. "Do not worry, Shefira. Our warriors have arrived at the front gates. The fight should be over soon."

A shadowy figure separates from the darkness. I stumble back a step, ready to run again, but the voice stops me.

"*Keeshla.*"

A cloud moves across the sky and the bright light of one of the moons shines down like a beacon on Zander. He's covered in green blood again, but the relief on his face is evident. Without thinking it through, I rush forward and throw myself into his arms.

CHAPTER 13

Holding London in my arms is like nothing else, although I wish it was not due to the current circumstances. When the call came through our chain of scouts that the Krijese were attacking the human settlement, fear I have not felt since I was a kit roared through me. I ran out of the village, gathering warriors as I went, and then took to the trees as soon as I reached the forest boundary. Anything to get to my mate faster.

I reluctantly draw back only enough to check and make sure she is not injured.

The liquid called tears, which I learned about from the healer's apprentice, spills from her eyes. I cradle her face between my palms and wrap my tail around her waist. "You are not harmed?" *Please do not be so.*

London shakes her head as much as my hold will allow. "No. Remi bashed the guy who grabbed Sage. After that, we were able to sneak through the side gate where your friend found us."

I glance over her head to find her four tribe sisters, including the healer's apprentice, standing beside Rojtar. Remi stands tall and holds her training staff in her hands. Even from this distance, the stains of her bloodied bandages are evident. She must be in great pain, although her expression does not show it. Still she holds her weapon ready to defend her people. Oh yes, she will make a mighty warrior and a fine mate for someone.

"Rojtar, while the other males are taking care of our enemies inside, we must get my *keeshla* and her tribe sisters to safety." I want nothing more than to join in the fight, but I must think of my mate's safety over my need to spill the blood of my enemies for daring to threaten her.

He crosses his fist over his chest. "Yes, Shefir."

I turn my attention back to London. "You will return to my village with us. It is not safe for you to stay here."

She steps away from me, so I loosen my tail's hold on her. I hope she does not try to argue. Her tribe sisters move closer, and she turns toward them. The four of them glance at each other but do not speak. They shift their gaze to my *keeshla*. Unspoken words must pass between them, because she faces me again.

"Okay, we'll go."

Thankful she has agreed, I wave them forward. Rojtar takes up the rear to make sure we keep the females protected between us. We cross the field and enter the forest. Our pace is swift, although much slower than my trek here. They all do their best to keep up, until finally we reach the clearing where our territory begins. I raise my hand to halt our progress. Behind me, the females breathe harshly, shattering the quiet night air.

I turn to address them. "We will reach our village soon. Once we arrive, the healer's apprentice will take Remi to the healer's tent to have her wounds looked after. One of our females will direct you to where you may sleep tonight. Tomorrow, we will help you set up your own dwelling."

The females nod, and when I walk forward, they follow, until the call of the mellenje breaks the silence. I return the sound, and from the shadows of the fiku trees beyond us, a figure steps out. He shows our sign of respect and nods as we pass. We break through the small grove of trees and the village spreads out before us. I can breathe easier with the knowledge that we are within the safety of our home.

The two guards at the gated entrance greet us. Their eyes widen at the humans behind me and follow us with their gazes when we walk past. I release another call of the mellenje, and two females come rushing forward to meet us part way to the central fire.

"The healer's apprentice will take the injured female to the healer. Please provide the others with furs for sleeping. Until tomorrow, they can sleep in the supply tent."

"Yes, Shefir." They dip their heads and gather the human females with soft whispers.

The six of them move away from us, although two of the human females glance over their shoulder at London, who attempts to follow. I wrap my tail around her waist to stop her. If only I could keep her in my embrace always. She jerks and gazes up at me with a wrinkle between her eyes as well as a question in them.

"You will sleep in my tent."

She opens her mouth and I tug her against me, which has her promptly closing it again. I nearly groan in pleasure as her hands rise to my chest, and my mating marks burn and flare to life. Her gaze drops to them before she lifts it to meet mine. "You are my *keeshla* and will become the Shefira of our village. My tent is where you belong and where you will sleep."

London narrows her eyes, drawing herself up tall. "Just because I agreed to come here, doesn't mean I agree to this whole fated mate business. I want to stay with my friends."

"It is late. We will discuss things in the morning after we've rested." I keep my tail wrapped around her and guide her in a different direction than the females took her tribe sisters.

She briefly attempts to head the same way they did, but my tail is still wrapped around her and curls further, which only brings her closer to me. She growls and smacks it with no more force than a strong wind, and I have to hold back my smile. I'm sure my mate would not like to be told she sounds like a dhembe kit. Finally, London ceases her resistance and allows me to lead her to her new dwelling. Despite her arguing, I will convince her our tent is where she belongs.

At last we reach it, and she pauses outside. Does she approve? I believe she will be even more pleased with the inside. I open the flap and gesture for her to enter first. She steps past me and her breath catches. I close it behind me, leaving us with only the light from the banked fire that burns low. My chest is tight with nerves and anticipation as London slowly turns in place, her gaze traveling around our home.

The large pile of furs on top of the stuffed sleeping pad are still in disarray from my hasty departure earlier. My own personal bathing tub sits empty to one side. Several trunks are lined up along the other side. There is one filled with leg coverings as well as other personal items. Another holds weapons Benham has made over the years, including one of my first swords and a few daggers. The few remaining belongs of my baba's and nene's are stowed carefully in a third, along with a few pretty coverings she crafted herself before she died, as a gift for my future Shefira. Will London like them? They are far different than what she currently wears.

"There is fresh water in the basin on the table if you would like to wash up before we sleep. A cloth should also be beside it," I say, unable to bear her silence any longer. "Tomorrow I will have the bath filled for you with heated water that you may enjoy."

Heated baths were my nene's favorite thing. Baba would draw her one every day, and he would allow no one to disturb her while she laid in it. If they please London, I will have one drawn for her every day as well.

She stops circling and faces me. "Thank you."

I nod, and without waiting on whether she chooses to wash up or not, I cross the distance of my tent and return my sword to the weapons' trunk. Behind me, there's a small splash of water. Needing to wash as well, I join London, who is wiping off her face. Droplets of water have spilled onto her chest covering, wetting it enough that the faint outline of her nipples are visible. Beneath my leg coverings, my cock stirs. Doing my best to ignore it, I grab a second cloth and wash away the Krijese blood from my flesh, nearly scrubbing myself raw as a distraction from the pleasing view.

Once finished, I set the cloth on the table. London does the same. I need to go speak to our scouts and advise them to send word when our warriors return.

"I must go take care of a few things regarding the males that remained fighting at the human settlement. Sleep, and I shall return shortly."

London opens her mouth as though to argue, but she closes it and sighs in resignation and nods. She moves to the mattress and bed pad and crawls beneath the furs, bringing them up so only her head is visible. The sight of her lying there with the knowledge that I'll join her soon makes my cock stir again. Before I can neglect my duties, I turn and step outside.

Several guards wander around the village, alert to any danger. One stands at attention outside the weapons tent. I stride through the village, past the central fire, until I reach the front gates and the two warriors standing guard. "Any word from the human settlement?"

"The Krijese have been defeated, Shefir. Your brother has ordered several of the warriors to dispose of the bodies and reinforce the entrance enough to last until daylight. The rest, including Zydon, are returning."

"Did we lose any warriors?" It's always my fear.

He nods gravely. "Two. They are being brought back for a proper burial."

My heart sinks at the news. We will be sure to give them a proper Tavikhi warrior celebration to lead them to Deeka. "Thank you."

They both place a fist on their chests, and I make my way back to my tent. I push aside the flap and step inside. The fire has burned even lower. With a skill born from habit, plus an increased ability to see in the dark, I cross over to my furs and climb under them to join my mate. Is it my imagination or do they already smell like London?

When I close the distance between us and drape my arm over her waist, she stiffens.

"Only sleep, my little mate. I promise you have nothing to fear from me," I assure her with a quiet whisper.

Slowly, she relaxes, but only slightly. She remains far too rigid, but at least she is within my arms. I close my eyes, inhaling deeply of her sweet scent that mixes with the fragrance of the livando bundles that hang from the wooden supports above. Peace settles within me. Never could I have imagined having my *keeshla* here. But this is where she belongs.

CHAPTER 14

London

I lie awake even after Zander has fallen asleep. His soft breathing comes from behind me, warming my skin with each exhale. I should be exhausted. I *am* exhausted, but I can't bring myself to close my eyes. The entire day comes rushing back, from hauling logs and water to cooking to the fear that slammed into my chest at the first scream that split the air. God, I hope everyone is all right.

When Zander appeared by the river, I'd been relieved. If it had only been me, I'm almost positive I would have agreed to come without any hesitation, based on nothing more than his promise to keep me safe. I'd never known fear like I did tonight when the Krijese attacked the settlement, but it was a decision we all needed to make together. What I hadn't expected was to be sharing a tent—a *bed*—

with him. I'd been too tired to put up much of a fight. All I wanted was a nice, comfortable place to sleep where I didn't have to worry about someone attacking me. Not that this village is infallible, but being surrounded by warriors capable of protecting us makes the worry a little less.

Except lying here—wide awake—I'm far too aware of the man whose chest I'm pressed against and whose arm is wrapped loosely around my waist. Whose tail twines between my legs and wraps around my ankle. This is the first time I've ever slept with a man. None of the guys back on Earth wanted anything to do with the lonely outcast with the dying mother. Even those who were just as poor as we were.

It's…nice being in Zander's arms. But tomorrow, I have to find the strength to leave his tent and find my friends. I shouldn't, rely on other people to take care of me. Almost as if he senses where my mind has gone, his hold tightens around me. The warmth of his skin seeps through the thin barrier of my loose-fitting sleep shirt. I'm also pretty sure the hardness pressing against my ass is exactly what I think it is. Why does being held by him have to feel so good? As though he'll take care of me, just like he said. *No.* I have to resist.

"Why are you not sleeping, my *keeshla*?" Zander's gruff voice whispers in my ear.

I startle. "You're awake."

He nuzzles my neck, rubbing his nose across it, and breathes in deeply. "You smell sweet, like the leaves of the lulebore plant."

A shiver cascades down my spine at his touch, and before I can stop myself, I press more fully into him. His lips curl up against my skin and then he's placing soft kisses along the slope of my shoulder. I tilt my head to give him better access before I realize what I'm doing. My brain is fighting with my body, but it's a losing battle.

Zander shifts his hand from my waist, sliding it higher until he's palming my breast, kneading it gently. I gasp, because something soft and ticklish is ghosting feather-light touches across my belly and dipping beneath the waistband of my shorts. *Oh god, is that his tail?*

So many sensations bombard me that I'm overwhelmed by them all. He must sense it's becoming too much, because he draws the appendage out from beneath the fabric and lets it twine around my calf and far away from my center. Still, he continues the sensual assault on my breast, tweaking and tugging my nipple. Arousal shoots right through me, and a tingling sensation grows stronger deep down inside my core. I clench my legs together, hoping to ease the pressure that's building, and trap his twitching tail between them.

"Your chest mounds are sensitive," Zander whispers hotly into my ear.

I can only nod, lost in a pleasure that's new to me. I've touched myself a few times, but none of them made my whole body light up like his does. His lingering kisses continue, heating my flesh and making me burn with a desire so hot it scares me. A small whimper spills from my lips.

"I have you, little mate. Just feel the pleasure I can bring you. The pleasure you bring *me*. We fit together perfectly. Just as Deeka intended."

Zander's husky declaration spears through me while his expert touch continues to wring every ounce of glorious ecstasy from my body. As though out of instinct, I press my backside more fully against him, needing something to ease the ache that's been slowly building since the first brush of his lips over my skin.

Just for tonight, stop overthinking. Stop holding back and enjoy everything he's doing. My mind finally gives up control and lets the sensations take over. The floodgates open. I cry out. "Touch me, please."

He gives one last gentle squeeze to my breast and then Zander glides his hand down my stomach. I flinch at the touch. He pauses only briefly, and when I don't demand he stop, he continues the lazy, and much too slow, trek downward. With only the slightest bit of teasing, he drags his fingertip along the edge of my waistband, taunting me with what's to come.

My breathing increases until, at last, he dips beneath the elastic. A streak of fire sizzles across my skin, burning hot. That heavy throbbing and tension low in my belly grows. My head is swimming. Finally, Zander touches me where I need him most. *Am I different from the females in his tribe?*

Does he like my body? The questions disappear like smoke when his finger grazes my clit. My hips buck, and I draw in a sharp breath. *God, yes. Don't stop.*

"What is this little piece of flesh?" More pressure is exerted against the sensitive nerve bundle and a shudder courses through me.

"It's called a clit," I gasp out, not even sure how I'm capable of speech.

"This pleases you?"

Afraid he'll stop what he's doing, I nod frantically. Zander chuckles and the sound vibrates against my neck, which only adds to the blissful feelings swarming in my belly. He changes up the way he touches me, repeating each one that makes me squirm and gasp. Tension builds and my body tightens. I blow out a breath and sparks fly behind my closed eyes. I shudder, crying out, and my pussy clenches down on emptiness. A few more flicks across the swollen flesh, and another orgasm rocks me.

Zander drags his finger along my still tingling clit, bringing forth another shiver before sliding his hand back up my belly, where he leaves it. I'm tugged closer, although I'm not even sure how that's possible since it's already as though we're melded together. The hard bar of his cock pushes right against my ass, but he doesn't take things further between us. He merely holds me close as my chest stops heaving and my breaths come slower until I'm breathing normally again.

I shiver and Zander brings up the furs that slipped down our bodies while he had his way with me. My cheeks heat.

I can't believe I let him do that. Yet I also can't find it in myself to regret it. *You deserve to feel pleasure after all the pain you've been through.* That small, selfish part of me I keep buried wants to take what he gave me and hold it close.

"Will you sleep now, *keeshla*?"

"You still believe in this fated mate stuff?" I can't help but ask, because it just doesn't seem possible, no matter what Zander says. *Are you sure?*

"Of course. It is how Deeka has always blessed her people. My mating marks are proof. Only our true mate can unlock them and make them burn and darken our skin. There are many warriors in our village who have longed for a mate, myself included." There's a hint of sorrow in his tone. "At least until you arrived on our planet. With only a single touch, our goddess has shown me that we are fated to be together."

I lie there absorbing his words. Of the warriors who have been at the settlement since our arrival the day before yesterday—*my god, was it really only two days ago?*—and this morning when they came to train the men, only a few have darkened marks on their skin. The remaining ones only have pale designs that run along their arms and torso. Could it really be some divine intervention that matches these men—aliens—with the one person they're meant to be with?

A sudden yawn escapes, and the exhaustion that had been eluding me earlier comes crashing through my body. It's a struggle to keep my eyes open, despite wanting to continue this conversation. Zander must sense the overwhelming fatigue threatening me.

"Sleep, London."

His softly spoken words drift over me, warming me, as slumber wins out.

CHAPTER 15

ZANDER

I wake to find my mate facing me and pressed tightly against my side with her arm resting on my chest and her leg flung over mine. London's long, flowing hair pools around her head. Her lips are slightly parted as she breathes softly and evenly. Pride swells in my chest as the memory of last night and the pleasure I was able to give her returns. My cock is still hard even after sleep. Of course it is. How could it not be with my sweet, little mate lying in my arms all night?

Not long after she'd fallen asleep, the call of the mellenje whistled through the village, signaling the return of our warriors. As much as I want to remain with London wrapped in my arms, I need to check on my brother and the rest of the males, including the two who lost their lives. My hope is that there are no mates to mourn them as they would soon follow them to the land of our goddess. Losing the males is sorrowful enough.

Careful not to disturb her, I slide from beneath London's tender hold and quietly move around our dwelling. I splash water on my face and chest and dry off with a cloth. I'll ask one of the females to bring in fresh water and clean cloths for when my mate wakes. My gaze lands on the trunk filled with the female coverings Nene made.

I open it and study the contents before withdrawing a delicate covering similar in color to my skin. Will she wear it for me? Hopeful, I close the lid and lay it on top so she will see it when she wakes. With a final glance over my shoulder, I exit the tent.

The village is busy with morning activities as everyone awakens and goes about their tasks. The fire is going strong, its flames reaching toward the sky, and several females stand next to it cooking our meal. Warriors walk to and fro, each intent on their destination, although the ones who spot me greet me with a nod. We have hunted enough over the last few days that our food stores are full, which gives the males time to practice their fighting skills in the arena at the base of the hill.

"I hear there are human females in the village, including your mate." My brother comes to stand beside me.

I move away from my dwelling so as not to disturb London. Zydon follows.

"They escaped through the side gate of the settlement during the fight. Rojtar discovered them alone by the river. It wasn't safe for them to remain."

"So you brought them here," he says, his tone bland and unreadable.

"They all agreed it was best."

He huffs out a small laugh. "It would seem you got your wish after all. Having your mate here in our village."

I glance over at him. He turns his head toward me and there's a hint of amusement in his eyes and one side of his mouth is curled in a smirk. A tightness in my chest unfurls. Despite sharing a womb and our close bond, there are still things Zydon and I disagree upon. I am glad this is not one of them.

He claps me on the shoulder. "I am truly happy that your mate is here with you. If anyone can convince her to remain, it is you."

I study him. "Have you considered that one of the human females might also be your *keeshla*? If Deeka has blessed me, then surely there are others she will bless as well."

Zydon doesn't respond. He merely continues walking toward the arena. I quickly catch up. "Do you not want a mate?"

This is not something we have ever spoken of between us. Our wishes for the goddess to provide us with our other half. I believe we both had begun to believe if we hadn't been sent her by now, we never would. At least that is how

I've felt. *Please accept my apologies, Deeka, for ever doubting you.*

"I do not know," he says after a moment's silence. "I was always envious of Baba and Nene's bond. Perhaps I have hoped for one, but with each season that has passed, I resigned myself to the fact that the goddess means for me to travel through this life alone."

Surely she doesn't? Zydon is a fine male. An even better brother. There are few more deserving of a mate than him. "I will send up prayers on your behalf that you find yourself as lucky as I, with a mate who is sweet and kind and beautiful."

"Thank you, brother." He picks up one of the training weapons near the perimeter of tightly packed ground that serves as our sparring arena and turns to me with a daring gleam in his eyes. "Care to take me on?"

My lips quirk as I reach for my own weapon and stride to the inside of the large area where we face off. In this, we are well-matched. In fact, Zydon, Zedam, and I, plus Benham, were the best warriors in the tribe growing up. Which is why I will never understand how someone, or who, defeated Zedam. It's the only explanation for the blood and his sword we'd found.

A hard thud cracks against my legs as my feet are swept out from underneath me. I land roughly on my back, the wind pushed out of my chest on a deep groan. Shaking off the confusion and pain, I glance up at Zydon who stands over me.

"Distractions will land you on your tail."

With a heave, I springboard back onto my feet and level a strike that he easily blocks. He then counterstrikes, but I jump away before his weapon can meet its target. We circle each other, come together, our weapons crashing together with so much force, the sound echoes through the air. I land a blow to Zydon's side, and he growls in frustration.

On and on, the sparring match continues as the sun rises mid-way to its zenith. Neither of us has taken the lead until, finally, my brother's weapon hits mine with enough jarring force that I hesitate a fraction too long before attempting to block his next strike. Once again, I find myself on my back on the ground, the dry dirt kicking up in a puff of dust around me. I lie there a moment, catching my breath, until a shadow covers me.

Zydon stands over me with an outstretched arm. I grip his wrist and he hauls me to my feet.

"Excellent match." My brother's grin matches mine. I clap him on the shoulder as one of the older kits comes over to take the weapons from us and return them to where the rest sit. My body aches in a way that says I've fought hard.

"Indeed. Let's go wash the dirt and blood off before you return to your mate. You don't want her to see you battered and bloodied by your younger brother."

I merely shake my head. Let him have his amusement. The next match is mine. "I assume all the injured males have been taken care of?"

"Yes. The few that received the worst injuries were left with the healer. They will be well in no time."

"I will be sure to visit them later." That is good news, at least. Sorrow fills me. "And the dead? Were either of them mated?"

"No, but one of them was Djale." Zydon's grief is evident.

My heart sinks. He had only seen twenty warm seasons. Barely older than a kit. "We will celebrate their lives tonight and mourn them for eternity."

A grief-filled silence settles for a moment.

"After we were able to help repair the front gate of the human settlement, I spoke with their leaders before I returned to our village," Zydon says, breaking it. "More than ten of their people were killed last night, including an elderly female. Two warriors remained behind in case the Krijese returned."

"Fuck."

"Our enemies are going to continue until there are no humans left." Zydon's tone is grave.

We have done everything we can for them. Offered our protection and to train their people to fight. "Let me think on this." I haven't felt this helpless since Zedam went missing.

"Shefir. Shefir." Young Talek runs toward us. He comes to a skidding stop, nearly colliding with me. He stares up, his eyes wide and his face full of awe. "Is it true there are human females in the village?"

Zydon and I share an amused glance, pushing away the conversation from moments ago. "It is true."

"How did they get here?"

I squat down to his level. "Rojtar and I brought them here to keep them safe. The Krijese attacked their settlement last night."

"Where are the rest of them?" Talek glances around as though they should be here.

"They remain in their home. Only five females accompanied us, including my mate." I pause, a solution brewing in my mind.

He bounces on his feet, his tail twitching excitedly behind him. "Your mate? I would like to meet her."

I chuckle and stand. "Let us wash up and then we shall see if she's awake."

Talek follows Zydon and me to the river where the three of us splash water over our bodies, rinsing away the dirt that has covered our skin. Once we're clean, I turn to the young kit. "Come."

We walk toward my tent.

"I am going to check in with the elders who are preparing for tonight's burial." My brother brings his fist to his chest and heads off in another direction.

The kit and I make our way through the village. He easily keeps up with my long strides, but mostly because he is nearly running. At last, we reach my tent. I raise my hand, signaling him to wait, while I push open the flap and step inside. My gaze is drawn to the empty bed furs. It would seem my little mate has wandered off. I can only assume in search of her tribe sisters.

I exit our dwelling. Talek's excited expression falls. That must be what one looks like upon not finding your *keeshla* waiting for you. I lay my hand on his shoulder.

"Let us go find the Shefira."

CHAPTER 16

London

I snuggle deeper into the comfortable blankets and breathe in the scent of flowers with a hint of something more earthy. *I don't remember my tent smelling this good or my bed feeling this soft last night.* A jolt of lightning hits me and everything comes rushing back. Going to sleep in my own tent. The first battle cry closely followed by screaming. Rushing to get out of the gate and stumbling upon the Tavikhi warrior and…Zander.

My whole body grows hot, and my cheeks burn. While I don't regret what we did, I'm not sure how I am going to face him in the light of day. This isn't anything I've ever had to deal with before. Slowly, I turn my head to glance over my shoulder. The space next to me is empty. Pushing aside the disappointment, I crawl out from beneath the warmth and pause. It's toasty in here, unlike the chill I'd woken up to yesterday morning inside my own tent.

A fire burns in the center pit. Someone must have recently stoked it. *Please let it have been Zander.* I'm already embarrassed enough by what happened last night. Having another person in here besides him makes me want to crawl back under the furs and hide. I move across the hard-packed dirt to the table where I'd washed last night. Fresh water sits in the basin, as well as clean cloths.

Once I've wiped the sleep from my face, I start for the door. It's time to go find the girls. Except I come to a complete stop. Spread out across the top of one of the trunks is the most beautiful dress I've ever seen. It's a pale purple that I'm almost sure will complement Zander's skin tone. The bodice is made up of only two thin pieces that form an X to cover my breasts but leave the rest of my torso and back exposed.

Gorgeous beads of various shades of purple and blue are sewn along the outer edge of the two pieces and along the hemline of the skirt that, from what I can tell, would hit about mid-shin. Where did it come from? Is it laid out for me to wear? I close the distance and stop directly in front of it, only an arm's length away. Unable to resist any longer, I reach out and touch the soft fabric. It glides across my fingertips like a cloud. I quickly snatch my hand back, afraid of ruining it.

Even if Zander or another person left this for me, I don't dare wear it. Not just because I haven't washed properly. If I wear it, does that mean I'm agreeing to this whole mate thing? I want to be the one to decide that we truly are mates, not some dress. With a heart full of regret, I bypass it, my gaze lingering at its beauty, and push the flap aside to step outside and get my first glimpse of Zander's village and his people.

Rounded tents nearly twice the size of mine back at the settlement dot the same yellow-dirt ground that seems to make up this entire planet. A large fire burns a distance away. Various pots of different sizes hang over the flames. Several Tavikhi that appear to be female stand around them, stirring whatever is inside. Based on the scents that drift from that direction, it must be food. My stomach chooses that moment to rumble.

"Shefira, may I help you with something?" A beautiful Tavikhi woman, with long flowing hair so like Zander's and the rest of the Tavikhi warriors I've seen, slowly approaches. Her expression is open and friendly. She stops just in front of me and bows her head.

Is she talking to me? She straightens and stares at me expectantly. I guess she is.

"Um, hi, I'm London. I was hoping you could show me to where my friends are staying, please."

She smiles broadly. "Of course, Shefira. It would be my honor."

I follow her away from Zander's tent, which appears to be even larger than the ones scattered about. It makes sense if he's the chief that he'd have the biggest home. As we walk through the village, I can't help but compare it to our settlement. The atmosphere is so different here. It's weirdly warm and inviting. Aliens mill around performing various chores as opposed to everyone sticking to themselves and their own little area they've claimed.

To my surprise, several Tavikhi children run through the village, chasing each other as their laughter rings loudly. I can't help but smile at their small, thrashing tails. If I had to guess, they look to be maybe eight to ten years old. It's hard to tell, and I'm certainly no expert when it comes to children.

Turning to the female at my side, I take in her appearance. A simple band wraps around her chest. She doesn't have breasts like us, but there's no mistaking she's female. She also wears a long leather skirt that almost dusts the ground.

"Do you mind if I ask your name?"

She darts a glance in my direction, her yellow and purple eyes widening, before quickly glancing away.

"I am called Alanda," she says softly.

"It's nice to meet you, Alanda."

"Thank you, Shefira." She dips her head again, and we come to a stop in front of a tent about the size of Zander's. I pause next to her. She steps to the side and sweeps her arm toward the flap covering the entrance.

"Your tribe sisters are inside."

A desperate urge to talk to them rushes through me, and I say a quick thank you before smacking the flap door. "Let me in, you guys."

Rustling comes from the interior as well as muffled voices, and in seconds, the opening appears and there's Remi. As soon as her gaze lands on me, she throws her arms around me, squealing in excitement and hugging me tight. Then I'm tugged out of her embrace and into Zara's, Maeve's, and finally Sage's.

"Holy shit, are we glad to see you," Zara says.

"Me too."

There's a quiet throat clearing behind me, and I turn at the sound. My escort still stands there almost shyly, although her gaze darts over my friends. I gesture toward her. "This is Alanda. Alanda, these are my friends Remi, Maeve, Zara, and Sage."

They each give her a little wave and she bows her head briefly. "It is an honor to meet the Shefira's tribe sisters. If there is anything you need, please let me know."

"I'm going to hang out in here. Thank you for bringing me to see my friends."

"Of course." Alanda clasps her hands against her chest and walks away.

Zara grabs my arm and drags me inside their tent. "Get in here and tell us everything."

I glance around. It's completely different than Zander's. His is a home. This appears to be some type of storage unit. Several bundles of furs are lumped on the ground from where the girls slept. There isn't a fire, so it's chilly, and, for a second, I miss the warmth I'd just left.

"How are your hands?" I glance at Remi and the bandages wrapped around her.

"They're fine. Whatever stuff these Tavikhi use for healing works like magic. The blisters are almost gone and only a little tingling remains." She fists her hips. "But we're not here to talk about my hands. Tell us about you and this mate of yours."

My cheeks flush again and I hope they can't see my face clearly in the barely visible light that comes from a couple of torches speared in the ground at the center of the tent.

"Yes, tell us everything." Once again Zara tugs on me, this time down onto the furs where the rest of them settle and wait.

They're obviously not going to let this go. "There isn't anything to tell." Okay, so maybe that's not entirely true. "Um, Zander brought me to his tent. I washed off some of my grime, as did he. Then we slept."

The four of them stare at me. Even Maeve glares at me with suspicion. I shift on the furs and try not to appear guilty.

"So you're telling me that your hot alien boyfriend just went to sleep with you in his tent?" Remi cocks her head and her lips quirk.

It's one of the many reasons I got caught stealing back on Earth. I'm a terrible liar. "Okay, so fine, maybe there wasn't just sleeping. We washed up and he left to go do some chief business. We talked about this mate stuff a little and how he believes his goddess brought us together. That there are warriors here who long for a mate and who hope that she'll bless them like she has him."

There's a collective sigh from the four of them.

"That's so romantic." Sage surprises me. Not that I know her very well, but I'm not sure I would have pegged her for someone who would think that way.

"It's kind of sad, if you think about it." Remi stares at the ground. "There are clearly females here, and yet some of the guys still don't have mates? Does that mean they're going to be alone the rest of their lives? No wife or husband? Do they not have casual hook-ups here? It just sounds lonely, I guess."

We're all quiet while we process her words. I hadn't thought of it that way when Zander had said that some of his people wanted mates. Don't they believe in friends-with-benefits? What about relationships without the whole mate marks and fate stuff? It's no wonder he's accepted it without question. The question is though, can I?

"Well, I don't know about you guys, but I have to pee." Zara stands and stares down at us. "I think we should go explore this new home of ours. Find some breakfast. Meet the locals. See what these folks are really like."

This is the bold Zara we met on the ship. Not the one who doesn't think she's any good at anything. I'll have to admit, I really kind of like this version of her. Taking our cue, we all stand as well. If I'm supposed to be the mate of the Tavikhi chief, I suppose I can't hide in here forever.

I lead the way out of the tent and don't make it two steps before I come to a grinding halt. One of the girls collides with me and I stumble forward, landing right in Zander's arms.

"You were right, Shefir, your mate does not have a tail."

CHAPTER 17

ZANDER

Once again, my mate is in my arms. I chuckle at Talek's announcement and set London on her feet. She takes a step away and her cheeks turn a brighter shade that matches the color of manerrat berries. I try to withhold my disappointment that she is not wearing the covering I left out for her. I glance over her shoulder to find her tribe sisters flanking her.

"Good morning. I hope you all fared well last night." I place my hand on the kit's shoulder. "This is Talek. He desired to meet you all."

London's gaze darts to the young male and then back to meet mine. There's an expression on her face I can't read. "Is this…is this your son?"

Ah, perhaps she is worried that there may be another female in my life. "No. Talek's baba is one of our hunters, and his nene helps make and repair coverings for our tribe members."

Being the fearless kit that he is, he breaks away from me and steps directly in front of London and stares up at her. "Hello, Shefira. It is an honor to meet you." He pauses and leans slightly around her before standing upright again. "Since you do not have a tail, you will have to ask Shefir to teach you another way to climb through the trees."

A beautiful smile lights up my mate's face and her tribe sisters all laugh softly. London quickly glances at me before placing her gaze back on Talek. "I will have to do that. And it is an honor to meet you as well."

"Alright, young one, why don't you go check in with your baba and see if he will be heading out to hunt today."

"Yes, Shefir." He nods and takes off running.

"Until I left the tent earlier, I didn't realize there were children in the village," London says.

"Talek is one of the last. There have been no new mated pairs or kits born in many seasons. We are the first." Which is something to be celebrated. "I am sure you all are hungry. The morning meal is soon. Many gather around the central fire and eat together. Please, join us."

One of London's tribe sisters steps forward with a hand raised. "Excuse me, but we need to know where we go to relieve ourselves first, if you don't mind."

"Ah, yes, forgive me." I direct them to the private area. "I will wait over there and escort you to our gathering place."

The five of them rush off and quickly return.

"Come." To my great pleasure, London walks beside me while her tribe sister's follow a short distance away.

We make our way to the central fire, and I glance over at my mate. "You did not wear the covering I set out for you." *Have I hidden my disappointment well?*

She bites at her bottom lip, drawing my attention to it. I want to press my own to hers as I understand the humans do as a show of affection. Perhaps I should have paid more attention to the healer when he relayed stories told to him by his human apprentice.

"I wasn't sure I should."

"Why is that?" Is there some human custom I am unaware of regarding a male giving a gift to a female?

"I didn't know what it would mean if I wore it," London says softly. "You know, like, was I committing to something?"

A tiny prick of pain pierces my heart. Not only that she didn't wear it, but that she thinks I would trick her into a mate bond with me. "While I will admit it was made by my nene for my future *keeshla*, I do not want you to think that any gift I give you comes with expectations. I merely thought it would look beautiful on you."

She places a hand on my arm and stops, making me pause as well. "I'm sorry. It is very beautiful, and I wanted to wear it. Thank you for the gift."

I bow my head and we continue on our trek until we reach the central fire, where more of our tribe brothers and sisters have arrived. There are many stares and whispers as they lay eyes on the humans. For some, this is the first time they've seen any. The females do not shrink away from the blatant curiosity, although the smallest of them, as well as the healer's apprentice, remain at the back. The bold one with hair color similar to ours and the one called Remi stand tall next to my mate at the front.

I step to the head of the fire. "Greetings. Let us welcome our new tribe sisters to the village."

Rumbles of welcome ripple through the village members present until everyone resumes their tasks. Meals are passed around and seats are taken. Discussions of tribe life, hunts, and preparation for the cold season reach me. Once I make sure that London has gotten her meal, I invite her to sit with me on a log bench. She glances at the other females, and the bold one waves her on as they wait to get their morning meal.

We sit in silence and eat. Although I am happy to be in her presence alone, the need to know her is strong.

"Is the food to your liking?"

She swallows and rests her serving tool in the bowl. "It's delicious. Different than what I'm used to, but it's good."

"What type of food do humans eat?" Considering how poor their hunters are, I am very curious.

"Back on Earth, there are machines that produced our food. We would push a few buttons and it would create it. Well, if you were wealthy enough to own one, that is."

This concept of a machine providing food is not one I can even picture, no matter how hard I try. I tip my head at the way she says this though. "And did you not possess this wealth?"

London laughs with a hint of bitterness. "Not hardly. It was just my mom and me. My dad left before I was even born. She did the best she could, worked a few jobs, but where I come from, it's hard enough to take care of yourself, let alone a kid. All she could afford, and barely that, were the standard protein bars. After she got sick, it was up to me to look out for both of us. Then she died."

"I am sorry for the loss of your nene." The grief of my own's death still lingers despite her having been gone for many moons. "Is that why you came to Tavikh?"

She lifts and drops both shoulders. "Basically. There was nothing left for me on Earth. I thought coming here would give me a fresh start. A new life different from the one I had. Of course, no one told us about the killer aliens who lived here."

It is as I suspected. The human leaders appear to not care about the people they send to our planet. "Well I am glad that you are here."

London turns her head in my direction and our eyes meet. Her smile is small, but it is present. "I am too."

Her words make my heart soar. We return to our meal, and still her tribe sisters have not joined us. I scan the area and find them sitting together, although they are also joined by Kyler, our healer. A shadow grows along the ground at my side until the male it belongs to sits on a bench next to us.

"*Keeshla*, this is my brother, Zydon."

London smiles politely, although her gaze bounces between us and her eyes widen slightly. "It's nice to meet you."

He nods. "You as well, sister."

Her surprise at his appearance is not unusual. Womb brothers are rare. Ones who are nearly identical to the other? Even more so. There is only one other set of womb brothers in the village, and they are among the few remaining elders.

"I thought to give London and her tribe sisters a tour of our village. Would you like to join us?" I haven't given up the idea that perhaps one of the other females could possibly be my brother's—or any of our other warriors'—*keeshla*. Fate and the goddess brought them here for a reason.

"Thank you for the offer, but I am to meet Jodah to go through our food stores. Make sure we are ready for the cold season. It will be upon us soon."

The past few cold seasons have been difficult for us. The Krijese have slaughtered many of the animals we hunt and left them bare of only their fur. They let the rest of the animal go to waste. While the meat had been spoiled by the time we came upon them, we were still able to use some of the remains, like the fat and bones. With the addition of the females—and perhaps additional humans—we will need to be even more prepared.

"This is good, although we should increase our stores as much as possible. I will return to the human settlement this day and make sure their gates have been fully fortified." I had given much thought through the night about what to do about the humans left there. "I will also offer, for any humans who wish to, the opportunity to join our tribe. As you said, the Krijese will not stop their attacks, and it is no longer safe for the humans to stay where they are. If they choose, they may come here."

Because we can easily read each other's emotions, Zydon does not need to tell me how he feels about this decision. I can sense his disapproval easily enough. However, he doesn't argue with me in front of my mate. He has never questioned my decisions publicly. No doubt he will approach me later when we are alone.

"Yes, Shefir."

I wince at the title. He only uses it when he's especially irritated with me. Zydon stands and leaves me alone with London, who turns to me again.

"Are you really going to let everyone stay here?"

I dip my head. "Those who wish to, yes." I don't tell her that I don't expect many to come. But at least I will have done my best to protect them. If they choose not to accept that help, then I will leave them be.

Noticing that she has finished eating, I take the bowl from her and rise. "I'd like to show you around our village, if you wish. After, we can return to our tent, and I will have a hot bath prepared for you."

London stands. "Can my friends come with us?"

"Of course."

Her beautiful lips tip up, and in that moment, I believe I would promise her anything, if only she would continue looking at me this way.

"Okay. Then yes, please. I'll admit to being curious."

I return the empty serving ware to the pile growing by the fire to be taken to the river for washing, and then we cross the distance to where the other females are still sitting. They all glance up at us as one.

"It would be an honor if you would join us as we explore the village."

"Shefir, Shefir." One of the warriors comes running, his tail thrashing behind him. "There is a Krijese at the edge of our territory. His weapons are sheathed and he appears to be alone. He says he wishes to speak with you."

My suspicions are raised, and my hand automatically goes to the sword at my hip. No Krijese has come this close to our village to try and engage in talk. All our previous attempts to speak with the Krijese leader in hopes of a peaceful truce have always taken place in neutral territory. What is this one doing here and why? I turn to London.

"I regret that I will not be able to accompany you at this time. I shall have one of the females show you around so you can become comfortable here." I place my fist on my chest and move to follow the male to where this Krijese waits, but London's hand on my arm stops me. I glance at her in surprise.

"You'll be careful?" she asks, her tone clearly full of worry, matching the flicker of fear in her eyes.

Closing the distance between us, I do what I have been wanting to since before the morning meal. I lean down and lightly press my mouth to hers. She startles but doesn't draw away. Wishing I could explore this lip touching more, I regretfully step back, breaking our connection. Without a word, I spin away, catching a brief glimpse of wonder on my mate's face, and take off to meet this unknown male waiting for me.

CHAPTER 18

When my mother died, I'd been terrified of life without her. As Zander hurries away, that same heart-pounding fear hits me. He has to be okay. Someone loops their arm through mine and rests their head on my shoulder.

"He's going to be fine." Remi's words of reassurance whisper in my ear. "He'll be back in no time. You'll see."

I can only nod and pray she's right. We stand there another minute while I let her comfort me, but then I gather myself. If I'm to be Zander's Shefira and his mate, then it's time I acted like it. I turn, and she loosens her hold on me so I can face my friends who've stood as well. "Let's take a look at our new home."

They all exchange glances and Remi, Zara, and Sage grin widely, while Maeve's smile is present but smaller. The expression is still new to her, but she's coming out of her shell a bit more every day. I glance around the central fire and find Alanda seated on the other side next to a male with the same dark-colored marks as Zander. He must be her mate. I head in their direction and stop in front of them.

"Hi, Alanda. I was hoping that if you weren't already busy, you wouldn't mind giving my friends and me a tour of the village. Zander wanted to before he was called away."

She glances sharply at the male next to her before staring up at me with the same expression as when I asked her name. Like she's stunned I would want to know anything about her or ask her for help. She swipes her hands down her thighs and quickly rises, bowing her head. "It would be my great honor, Shefira."

"Please, call me London. It's what all my friends call me."

"Oh, no, I couldn't." She shakes her head.

It's clear she's not ready for that yet, so I won't push. Instead, I just smile. "Maybe one day. And you're sure you're not too busy? I don't want to take you away from a prior obligation."

"Not at all." She glances back at the male still seated. "Oh, this is my mate, Rassim."

"It's a pleasure to meet you."

Rassim places his fist on his chest. "An honor, Shefira."

You better get used to it. I reach out and loop my hand around Alanda's elbow and draw her away with a small wave goodbye at her mate. We join the girls who are waiting for us.

"Alanda has kindly agreed to show us around." I loosen my hold on her.

We walk away from where everyone is slowly dispersing and getting on with their daily tasks. As we stride through the village, I take in the surrounding area just outside where the village stretches out. Behind Zander's tent is a large, grassy hill—mountain almost—that extends along the entire length of the horizon. Off in the distance, there appear to be small dots that decorate the side of it. I point in that direction.

"What are those little black things up in the hills out there?"

Alanda turns her gaze to where I'm pointing. "They are the dhibani that live there. Our hunters search them out because their hides are soft for making coverings and their meat provides us food. We also use their innards for storing water."

My stomach tosses a bit at that, but I swallow down the nauseated sensation that comes with it. This is our life and we're going to have to adapt to it. Although, maybe next time I won't be so quick with questions I might not want the answer to.

We continue walking through the village, passing by the supply tent where the girls slept, the weapons stores where a guard is stationed, as well as the food stores. Next we come upon a large dwelling nearly the size of Zander's.

"This is the healer's tent." Sage points it out. "His name is Kyler, and he's the one who has been teaching me about Tavikhi medicine. It's where I got that special salve for Remi's wounds."

"Oh my god, that stuff is like magic," Remi gushes holding up her hands and wiggling her fingers.

Out of nowhere, a small body rushes up to us. "May I join you, Shefira?" It's Talek.

"Are you sure it's all right with your mother and father?" I don't want to get him in trouble if he has other chores he's trying to avoid.

He nods. "Baba says he and I will go hunting tomorrow. There is still plenty of time before the cold season truly arrives."

"Then we'd love to have you." I'll admit, he's pretty adorable with his chubby cheeks and little tail. It does make me wonder what sort of things the children in the village learn besides hunting. Are there female children as well? Do they also hunt?

As we continue walking toward the river, Talek takes over for Alanda in telling us all about village life. The river is for bathing and washing. "I don't like bathing in the cold season. I'm worried my tail will freeze and fall off. Then how will I climb and leap through the trees?"

I glance over at my friends and they're all trying to hold back their laughter. I nod sagely, trying to be serious, because it's clearly a big worry for him. It does make me curious about all this tree leaping he's referring to though. Maybe I will have Zander show me.

"Tell me about this cold season." Do they get snow here? There were months back on Earth that the whole world was covered in it.

"It is truly terrible," he says in a dramatic way that only a child can. "The cold dust falls from the sky and covers the ground so high that I would get lost in it. Although, I have grown taller since the last cold season, so perhaps no longer."

My mouth gapes. They get that much? I glance at Sage.

"Did you know that?"

She appears as surprised at the news as me and shakes her head. "I've been here such a short time, I haven't experienced any other season since I arrived. I mean, it might have been a little cooler when I got here, but I can't remember."

Add it to the never-ending list of things we weren't told before arriving on the planet. No matter. We're here and we'll deal with it just as the Tavikhi have done. We turn from the river and circle around the outer perimeter of the village.

"This is where the elders live." *This* is a large grouping of tents standing close to each other, not far from Zander's.

They butt up against the hillside as well, and a smaller central fire burns between them all. An unusual earthy fragrance comes from the area and smoke dances upward from an opening in the roof of one of the dwellings.

Talek rushes ahead and then stops at the top of a rise, pointing down into a shallow valley. Groans and loud cracks reach me. I come to stand next to him and the rest of the girls form a line next to me as we all stare toward where the noise is coming from. At the bottom of the hill, Tavikhi warriors are paired off and fighting each other inside a large circular space. Some fight with staffs or swords, while others hold nothing but daggers. The power they exhibit is stunning and reminds me of the day we arrived and the Krijese attacked.

"This is where we train for battle." Talek stands straighter, his tail whipping wildly behind him. "One day I'm going to be a great warrior."

"I'm sure you will be." He certainly seems determined enough.

I continue standing there, admiring the warriors' skills. It's hard not to. All that muscle and strength. It's enough to make any woman take notice. I can picture Zander down there wielding his sword and taking down his opponent. The way he'd then turn in my direction and our eyes would meet, victory shining from his.

He'd stride forward, his power evident, and sheath his weapon without looking away from me until finally, he'd stop so close our bodies nearly touch. His tail would wrap around my waist, and he'd tug me tightly against him, swooping down and kissing me until I'm left breathless and panting. Then he'd carry me in his arms to our tent and ravish me throughout the night.

Shaking off the carnal thoughts, I clear my throat and quickly glance at my friends, hoping they can't read my mind. Thankfully, their attention is still down on the training area, except for Zara, who's staring at me with a knowing grin. Rather than be embarrassed, I chuckle and give her a little shrug. She wiggles her eyebrows up and down and blows me a kiss. I shake my head at her antics.

"Can you tell me how the village is run?" I direct the question to Alanda. "Who is responsible for what, I mean?"

Her ridged brow shifts in what I suspect is confusion. "We are all responsible for everything, Shefira. There are males and females who hunt. We have the males who rotate guarding the entrance. Some of the males scout the forest, keeping an eye out for the Krijese. The elders who are able to, help with cooking, while others make new coverings to last us through a couple cold seasons, especially the kits as they grow quickly. If someone is sick, another takes over for them until they get well. If a warrior is injured enough that he can't hunt or fight until he's healed, he will often help with other tasks."

I glance back toward the village. The Tavikhi really are a community that works together for the sake of everyone. It's so different than Earth, where those of us on the bottom rung struggle to even survive, with no assistance from anyone. Not even if we begged. And we've been lucky enough to have been accepted by these people. I take a deep breath and face Alanda.

"Show us what we can do to help."

CHAPTER 19

ZANDER

All around me, the forest is quiet. There are no mellenje calls or the skittering of tiny claws of the ketri who usually scurry along the ground beneath the fallen leaves of the fiku trees. It's like even the animals are wary of the beast that lingers nearby. Scouts are scattered throughout the trees, keeping watch from above for any more Krijese besides the lone one waiting for me a short distance away.

Slowing my approach, I keep my hand at my side near my weapon as a precaution. My ears twitch as I wait for any sounds indicating there are more than just the two of us. There is nothing. Only the heavy sound of his breathing reaches me. The protection of the trees ends and opens to a clearing where our enemy stands.

A long, wooden-handled blade is sheathed across his back, and there's a dagger secured at his hip. Otherwise, no other weapons are visible. His arms hang loosely at his sides. I come to a stop a fair distance away and scan the length of the field.

"There are no others waiting to ambush you, Tavikhi," he says in a guttural growl, his gaze traveling over me, no doubt taking in my mating marks. "It is only me."

That may be so, but I have learned not to trust the Krijese. "What are you called, and what is your business here?"

"I am Kushtar, and I come as an emissary on behalf of King Armik. We wish to propose a truce between our people."

Sharp suspicion rises at the request. Not once, even when his father was their leader, have the Krijese wanted peace. "What brings this change of heart?"

He pauses as though considering how much to share. "Our people are dying out."

This surprises me. "What of your females?"

"There are only a few left. Disease has taken many of them. We stopped having offspring many moons ago."

A burning flame of rage ignites. "And the human females you have stolen?"

"All dead." The way he speaks is as though it is of no consequence.

My hand goes to my sword, and I take a step forward. Kushtar shifts to a defensive stance and reaches for the handle of his blade. I stop. If he is here to truly seek a truce, I have to control my temper no matter how much it pains me to do so. I sneer at him. "You come here speaking of truce, and then tell me you have killed the human females you have stolen?"

"We killed no one." Kushtar's mouth slit widens and he snaps his teeth. "Some died trying to birth our offspring, while others chose to sacrifice themselves to their god."

This news sickens me. They force these females to bear their kits or cause them so much pain they end their own suffering? "And the kits?"

At last a flicker of emotion comes from him. "Also dead. Their blood was tainted by the humans, and they were too weak to survive."

"You propose a truce, and yet only last night you attacked the human settlement which is under our protection." For the moment, I keep silent that I have found my mate among them. "More than a dozen humans were killed as well as all of the tribe members your leader sent. Yet you dare stand before me wanting peace?"

Kushtar shakes his head. "We have only offered a truce to you. The humans are weak. We have no use for them. Even their females are useless."

I'm disgusted by our enemies and an instant denial climbs up my throat, but I can't be hasty in making a decision. Instead, I straighten. "You can tell your king that I will think on this. Return tomorrow at this time and he will have his answer."

Slowly, I retreat back into the forest, never taking my eyes off the Krijese in front of me, until I'm enclosed within the trees. Only then do I turn and make my way to the village. I trust my hidden warriors to alert me if the Krijese attempts to follow. At last, I cross the entrance and head toward my tent. Zydon and Benham are the first to greet me.

"What did he want?" My brother wastes no time.

More than anything, I want to search out my mate, but the safety of our people as well as the humans, must take priority. "Come, let us speak."

The three of us stride through the village and then enter my dwelling. I turn to them and relay everything I learned from the Krijese emissary. Benham growls and Zydon blows out a breath.

"So they want peace with us, but to continue waging war against the humans." My brother paces, his tail thrashing.

"It would appear that way."

He stops. "Did you tell him that you were mated to one of the human females?"

"My instinct said to not."

"Probably for the best." Zydon returns to pacing. "What have you decided?"

"How can I accept peace between our two tribes and yet allow the Krijese to attack my mate's people? Especially for those who do not choose to join our village."

Once again, my brother comes to a stop. He stares at me, incredulous. "You still intend to extend the invitation to the humans?"

"Of course. Even more so now with the threat the Krijese present to them."

Benham, who's remained quiet this whole time, speaks up. "While I still think the humans are weak, unskilled, and undisciplined, I find I cannot allow them to be senselessly slaughtered. If Zander feels it best that they join our tribe, then I support him in this. Although I do not know how this will affect the proposed truce."

While I admit my tribe brother has surprised me with his support, I do understand. Benham has a kind heart beneath his hard exterior. During our hunts, he always offers his thanks to his kills for the things they provide us.

"It does not matter. If the Krijese choose to withdraw their offer, then so be it. We will continue to protect not only our people, but my mate's, to the best of our ability as we have been doing since they arrived on this planet." It is as it should be.

Zydon sighs in defeat. "When will you approach the human leaders?"

"I will go after the mid-day meal, so I know what my answer will be when the Krijese returns tomorrow. Now, I would like to search out my mate."

My brother and Benham place their fists on their chests and exit my dwelling. Just as I am about to follow, the flap swings open and London comes rushing in. She pauses for a moment, her gaze taking me in, and then she runs forward and throws her arms around me. I return the embrace and breathe in her sweet scent. It soothes the windstorm of anger that swirls inside me.

"I'm so glad you're okay. I've been so worried."

My heart soars with my *keeshla*'s words. I twine my tail around her and draw back. London tips her face up and, unable to resist, I press my mouth to hers. It's wonderful, but almost as though there is something more to it that I'm missing. When her tongue darts out to flick across my lips, I raise my head in question. Her eyes open slowly and she blinks.

"Did I do something wrong?"

"This mouth touching. It involves tongues?" It was not unpleasant, but I'm not sure how it provides pleasure.

London giggles. "It depends on who you're kissing."

"Kissing? Is that what you call it? And who do you not use tongues with?" I'm fascinated by this.

She nods. "You only use your tongue with your mate. I've shared kisses with my mom, but those were on our cheeks. I also suppose you could share a cheek kiss with a friend too."

My brow ridges shift. "You do not know of these friend kisses?"

London's gaze darts from mine and grief surrounds her. "I didn't have any friends back on Earth. Remi, Maeve, Sage, and Zara are my first."

I study my mate. There seems to be much loneliness in her past. At least I had my brothers and Benham when I was growing up. "I am glad you have them now."

"Me too."

With a finger under her chin, I tip her head up again. "Perhaps we should practice more of this kissing then. So I get it right."

To my delight, it is my *keeshla* who presses her mouth to mine this time. Again, her small tongue flicks out and brushes across my lips. I part them and she grows bolder. Ah, so this is what was missing. I definitely see the appeal of this kissing. Letting her lead until I feel confident that I can provide her as much pleasure, I sweep my tongue alongside hers and then into her mouth, tasting her flavor that is as sweet as her fragrance.

London presses herself against me and I deepen the kiss, fusing our mouths together. My hand goes to her chest mound. She draws in a sharp breath but doesn't pull away from me. Taking several steps backward, I bring her with me until the stuffed bed pad touches my legs. Gently, I guide us both down until we're lying side by side. My mate is like all the stars and the moons in the sky. Perfect and beautiful.

"Let me bring you pleasure, *keeshla*."

London's eyes open slowly. They glow softly in the firelight. She nibbles on her kiss-plumped lip and nods. I tug the chest covering she wears up and she sits up long enough for me to slip it over her head. She lies back and her chest mounds, with their tips hardened, beg for my mouth. I close my lips over one and taste, flicking my tongue over the tight pebble. A breathy moan spills from my mate's lips. Pride swells in my chest that I am giving her this pleasure.

I give its mate the same attention and then drag my lips down her stomach until I reach her short leg coverings. Those I also remove, pulling them down her legs and tossing them aside. My eyes drink in the sight of her. There's a small patch of dark fur covering her cunt. The scent of her arousal is powerful and drives mine to match. I must taste her. Dipping my head, I swipe my tongue up her slit and lash it against the bit of flesh she called a clit. London clutches my head tightly, her fingers threading through my hair and her blunt claws digging into my flesh.

"You taste like the berries of the lengje plant. Sweet and juicy. I will never be able to eat one again without thinking of my mate's delicious cunt."

Above me, London whimpers. As much as I want to keep lapping up her flavor, my cock aches to slip inside her heat. I take one more taste and then quickly discard my leg coverings. Bringing my lips down to hers, I resume the mouth touching—kissing. My mate's fingers clutch my arms and my mating marks burn at her touch. The heat runs through my body and straight to my cock.

I reluctantly pull away and stare down at her, waiting for our eyes to meet. At last, London opens hers. They've darkened in color from the nenuphar plant to almost the color of the fiku tree. They're heavy with arousal.

"Tell me you are my mate," I nearly demand. "That you are the one Deeka has chosen for me above all others."

"I am your mate." It's only a whisper, but there is no hesitation and the sound of it washes over me with pleasure.

"And I am yours." With that, I place my cock at the entrance of her cunt and slowly push inside.

London is so tight around me, and I can't hold back my groan. She flinches slightly and I sink fully into her. Our lips meet and soon our tongues dance to the same rhythm as my cock thrusting in and out of her tight heat. The outside world disappears as well as any worries of truces. Inside our dwelling, it is only my *keeshla* and me.

Reaching between us, I circle her clit in all the ways I remember brought London the most pleasure. My mating nodes open and begin to secrete the fluid meant to increase her arousal. She throws her head back and her cunt clenches down on me. A scream tears from her throat and her body shudders. The rippling pleasure vibrates through me and my cock erupts, releasing my seed deep inside her. I collapse over her, our breaths harsh in the quiet of our dwelling.

Keeping us connected, I roll to my side, bringing her with me. I brush the damp hair off London's face and press a brief kiss to her lips. She shivers and I draw the furs over us.

"I did not hurt you?" I ask.

Slowly her eyes open and she shakes her head. "Only a little at first, but it went away quickly and felt good after that."

This is good. She had been so tight, I am not sure she had ever been with a male before. I am glad I gave her pleasure. We lie together in silence. I have obligations to attend to, but all of them can wait a while longer while I savor this closeness with my mate.

"Let us rest and then we will talk."

CHAPTER 20

We're still lying beneath the furs. I hadn't meant to fall asleep, but I'm awake now and tracing the mating marks painted across Zander's chest.

"What did the Krijese want?" I tip my head back to stare up at him.

His fingers pause in their gentle gliding motion along my arm. "He brought a proposal for a truce between our people. They are dying and have no wish to lose any more. As with us, they have not had any kits born in far too long, and they number even fewer in females."

It's hard for me to imagine those terrifying aliens actually having females. Are they as brutal as the males? I also can't help but feel a little sorry for them. Who wants their species to die out? "What did you tell him?"

"I have not decided yet. They have sworn no peace with the humans."

What? I sit up, dragging the fur with me to keep my chest covered. "What do you mean?"

Zander remains lying down, but his eyes stay on me. "They will not fight with us, but to them, the humans are weak and do not belong here. The Krijese said their leader will not stop attacking."

Sagging, I lie back down and curl closer to him, trying to warm myself. "So they'll keep killing humans, but leave the Tavikhi alone."

"Yes."

My belly hurts at the thought of all those innocent people being slaughtered. It's not right. But I don't know what the solution might be.

"I will be returning to the human settlement shortly, and as I mentioned at the morning meal, offering a place in our village to any human that wishes it."

"Truly?"

Zander nods.

"Can I come? Maybe I can convince more people to accept." I don't wish for any more people to die.

"You are the Shefira of our tribe. It is your right to be part of the decisions that affect us all."

Wow. That feels like a lot of responsibility. I'm not sure I'm prepared for it. Zander must sense at least some of my thoughts, because he places a finger under my chin and tips my head up. "Deeka chose you as my *keeshla* for a reason. She would not have given me someone unworthy of the position as my Shefira."

I swallow and nod shallowly. He releases me, and I rest my head on his shoulder again. A long silence grows between us. It's time he knows the type of person his Deeka chose for him. "I've never been a leader. Instead, I did what people told me to do. My whole life. But most especially after my mother died. Everything we had went to paying for her medicine. A lot of good that did, because she died anyway."

I swallow at the memory. It's still so fresh in my mind. "After she was gone, I was left with nothing. No food. No means to get any either. I didn't know what I was going to do until I was approached by a member of this street gang that lived in our neighborhood. They were nothing but criminals. He said my mother owed him money. She didn't though. I mean, she couldn't have. He told me that I had to start working for them to pay off her debt."

All I remember is the fear. There was no one I could go to for help. "Anyway, I didn't really have a choice. The first job they gave me was to steal this pocket watch from some fancy rich guy. I tried. Of course, I was caught red-handed. The police put me in jail. Apparently the rich guy wanted me punished. I was in there for two months before they took me before a judge. He gave me two choices. I could either spend the next fifty years in prison, or I could be shipped to some faraway planet. I chose Tavikh."

I hold my breath, waiting for Zander to condemn me. To realize that the woman his precious goddess picked as his mate is a thief and a liar.

"When I was near Talek's age, my youngest brother, Zedam, found a beautiful, sparkling rock beneath the water's surface one day when we were out exploring. I was envious that he had found it first. He picked it up and brought it back to our tent. The next morning, when he reached for it beside his furs, it was gone. He searched everywhere for it and his grief was strong. Several days later, our nene discovered me with it. I had woken in the middle of the night and taken it, because it was so beautiful that I wanted to add it to my collection."

Zander tips his head to glance down at me.

"You were a young female who was alone and hungry. I was merely a selfish kit who was disappointed something didn't belong to me. You will receive no judgment from me, my *keeshla*. I only hope you do not judge my actions too harshly."

I shake my head. "Of course not. You were just a little boy who made a mistake. I'm sure you made up for it."

He's silent a moment, his gaze distant and unfocused. "I tried to. At least until his death."

"I'm sorry you lost him."

"Zydon does not think him dead. But he has been missing for many lunar cycles with no word. If he were not dead, then why has he not returned?"

My arms tighten around him, hugging him hard. I can't imagine the pain of not knowing what happened to his brother. Zander shifts. "As much as it pains me, we must rise if we are going to make it to the human settlement and back before the sun descends."

I sigh, not quite ready to leave our tent, but knowing we must. We crawl out from beneath the furs, and he pulls his pants back on. I reach for my old clothes, but Zander stops me. "If you'd like to wash, I will get you something to wear."

While he goes to his trunks, I move to the basin of water at the table and wet a cloth before cleaning myself. Once I've finished and dried off, I turn. In his hands is a small bundle. I take it from him and smooth it out. It's two pieces, similar to what Alanda wore earlier although the top piece covers more. I slip the leather top over my head and step into the skirt, tying it at my waist.

"You are beautiful."

I glance up and Zander's eyes glow in the light of the fire. "Thank you for the dress."

"It is my honor that you wear it."

He takes my hand, lacing our fingers, and we step outside the tent. The sun is directly overhead and shines down brightly, taking some of the chill out of the air. The mid-day meal is already under way as most of the village is already gathered around the central fire. Zander leads us there and we quickly eat some type of root vegetable and meat.

"I'm going to let the girls know where I'm going and then I'll be ready."

He nods and I rush over to where they all sit in the same place where they ate breakfast.

"Zander and I are going back to the settlement to talk to Gary and Adam. We'll be back soon."

Remi sets down her bowl. "What's going on? Does this have something to do with that meeting he rushed off to with the Krijese dude?"

I nod. "We're inviting anyone who wants to, to come live in the village. It's no longer safe at the settlement."

Zara makes a noise. "You're not fucking kidding it isn't. Then again, was it ever?"

Probably not. "Anyway, we'll be back in a little while. I just wanted to let you guys know that I was leaving for a bit."

I glance up and Zander is waiting. "I'll see you soon."

"Wait." Remi jumps to her feet and comes over for a hug. "Stay safe, okay?"

"I will."

She releases me and I cast one last glance around my circle of friends and cross to where Zander is standing on the side of the fire nearest the front entrance of the village. He takes my hand again and we head off. As we walk through the small clearing and then into the forest, I take in my surroundings. Last night it was so dark, I'm not even sure how we made it through the trees without colliding into them.

The trunks are a coal black, which only makes the purple leaves that much brighter. The contrast between the colors is beautiful. Especially with the yellow dirt that is visible along the narrow trail. Other bushes and plants of various shades make up the forest floor. Birds of some kind call to each other and there's the occasional rustle of bushes from whatever critters live here. There's a tension in Zander as we walk, like he's alert for any danger that might jump out at us. I stay silent so as not to distract him.

There's another small break in the trees where a field lays, and then we're back under the canopy of the landscape. I'd estimate we've walked twenty minutes before I catch a glimpse of the settlement walls through a small gap between two large trunks. Zander holds up his hand and we pause just within the safety of the shadows of the forest. Moments pass with nothing happening and then finally, he motions for us to proceed.

We arrive at the gate that is barely hanging on. It's been roughly patched up, but it's not as though the Tavikhi could make it perfect in the middle of the night. I'm sure they did the best they could. Zander pounds on the gates. We wait several minutes before the right side creaks and groans as someone opens it. An unfamiliar man greets us.

"We're here to see your tribe leaders," Zander announces.

The man steps back and lets us pass. I get my first glimpse of the destruction and tears well in my eyes. Tents lay crumpled on the ground. The supply building door is missing, and metal boxes and other items lay strewn around outside of it. The central meeting house has been burned and half of it lays in a heap of rubble. That doesn't even begin to describe things. People walk around like ghosts, their faces either devoid of expression or with red-rimmed eyes and shoulders heavy with defeat.

Adam and Gary approach. Both have dark circles under their eyes, and their steps drag with what I can only imagine is exhaustion.

"Shefir." They both nod.

"We have come with a proposition for you and your people. The Krijese leader has approached me regarding a peace truce between our two tribes. They, however, have not extended the same to you. If any of your tribe members would like to leave your settlement and join our tribe, they will be welcome." Zander lays everything out. "They will be required to hunt and fight alongside us. They will also need to learn any other skills like tanning, weapon-making, food preparation, and anything else that our tribespeople do. Everyone is responsible for something to help village life run smoothly."

Gary and Adam exchange glances. "This is our home. Up until last night, we were doing just fine."

I step forward. "What about when the next ship arrives dropping off more humans, and the Krijese attack? Because they will. What are you going to do then? There are women and children here. You should let the families decide for themselves if they want to stay or come with us."

Adam stiffens, but Gary releases a sigh. "We'll have a meeting. They can choose."

"The Krijese will return tomorrow to learn if we accept their terms. If I do, then know that there is only so much we will be able to do to help you. We must protect our village and any newcomers who choose to join us."

"We will ask," Gary says.

While we wait, the two leaders gather all the people of the settlement outside the destroyed central meeting house. Murmurs rumble through the crowd as they all receive the news.

"Will you really leave the ones who stay to fend for themselves?" I can't picture Zander being that cruel.

He stares down at me. "Our people will not abandon yours completely, but they have to learn to defend themselves in some way. We cannot be here all the time. Our warriors must also make sure that our people, including those who join us, are fed and protected, especially if I do not accept the terms of the truce. Also, the cold season will be arriving and once it does, hunting becomes that much more difficult."

Zander is right. He has done the best he can. The humans should be doing more to protect their own people. The Tavikhi have offered sanctuary as well as training. We can't force anyone to do either of those things if they choose not to. Finally Gary and Adam return.

Gary wrings his hands in front of him. "The families with children, as well as a few others, have agreed to go with you. Everyone else says they'll stay here. Although the men would like to continue training with your warriors if the offer is still on the table."

Zander dips his head. "Of course. Training will continue as planned. I will have three or four of our warriors return in the morning."

"Thank you." This is from Adam.

"Please have the families who will be leaving pack up whatever belongings they wish to bring. I will send back several warriors after the evening meal to guide them to our village." Zander turns to me. "Are you ready?"

When he mentioned having the families pack their things, I remembered my books back in my tent. I hope they weren't destroyed in the attack last night. "There is something in my tent I would like to bring with me if it's still there."

"Of course."

I nod my thanks and run through the decimated settlement to where, for a brief time, my friends and I had put down our roots. None of our tents are left standing. Dread lands in my belly. Praying that they haven't been ruined, I manage to root through the remains of my former little space until I find what I'm searching for. Relief runs through me. I carefully pick up each book strewn across the ground and hold them tightly to my chest, breathing in their scent. Somehow in the mess, I manage to find my bag as well and tuck them inside. With a final glance around, I walk away and back to where Zander waits.

My mother always said that there was a time and season for everything.

"I'm ready."

He twines his tail around my waist, and we leave the settlement behind. Now is my time with my mate.

CHAPTER 21

Careful not to disturb my sleeping mate, I slide out from beneath the furs. I need to meet with the Krijese this morning. After quickly washing, I exit our tent. The moons still linger in the sky, but the sun is just cresting the horizon. My breath puffs out in bursts of smoke in the cold air. A few warriors wander through the village. Five families, including six kits and three elders, joined our tribe last night. In only two short days, we've grown by over twenty.

I make my way toward the entrance. Footsteps come from behind me. I turn to find Zydon heading my way.

"Will you be joining me, brother?"

"Someone has to guard your back." He claps me on the shoulder.

It's good to have him along. We have not spent nearly enough time in each other's company in recent days. I also still don't trust the Krijese emissary to come alone. We make our way quietly through the trees, not disturbing any of the animals who live among it. At last we come to the clearing. Zydon stays within the trees, keeping guard. As with yesterday, the Krijese appears to be alone.

"Have we come to an agreement, Tavikhi?" He comes straight to the point.

"We do not accept your terms."

The Krijese growls low, and his mouth slit widens, showing his teeth. "You are making a mistake."

"You are the one whose people are dying. I do not want to continue waging war with your tribe. But I cannot accept a truce that does not include the human settlement as well. If you were to amend the terms and leave the humans in peace as well, then we accept. Otherwise, we will continue protecting them against your people until none of you are left." While it pains me to destroy their species, I will do so if it means protecting my mate and her people.

"I will take your words back to my king." With another teeth-gnashing snarl, he pivots and takes off at a lope, no doubt to relay my message to his leader.

Zydon steps out from the trees. "Do you think they will stop?"

"I do not know. We can only hope for their sake that they do." I keep my gaze to where the Krijese disappeared a moment longer, and then start the trip back to our village and my mate. I did not like leaving her without a proper farewell. Rojtar and another warrior stand vigilant at the gated entrance, each one offering their respect.

My brother and I part ways, and I cross through the village and past the central fire where several females are preparing it. I reach my tent and step inside. The fire burns low, and the warmth of the interior takes the chill from my skin. London remains buried beneath our furs. The morning meal is still far enough away that I climb back onto the sleeping pad and curl my body around my mate's, wrapping my arms around her waist and my tail around her legs.

She wiggles closer and mumbles. "Did you go meet the Krijese already?"

I press a kiss against her bare shoulder, and she tips her head for to me run my lips up the side of it until I reach her ear. "I did."

"How did he take the news?"

"Not well. Said he would take my decision back to his tribe leader."

London moans as my wandering hand cups her chest mound. I tweak the rigid tip and she pushes herself harder against me. My cock, which had been hard the moment I pulled her into my embrace, hardens even more. I notch it between her legs, the wetness of her cunt already providing slickness for me to glide through.

"No more talking of our enemies while I'm trying to plea-sure my mate."

She rocks back and moans again as my cock head butts up against her clit. London tips her hips and on my next forward push, I slip inside her tight heat. A groan climbs up my throat. It's not enough. I shift our positions so she is face down and her hips are raised off the sleeping mat. She's spread wide open for me. My cock disappears deeper inside her cunt. I can't take my eyes off where we're connected as I pull part way out and push forward again.

"Oh god, I can feel you even more this way."

My pride swells that I can please my mate like this. I begin to thrust and each time, London rocks backward to meet me. My tail curls around and rubs her clit, stimulating her in the ways that bring her the most pleasure. Her wetness spills from her, coating it. The puckered back hole draws my gaze. I swirl my finger around its edges, not going any further, just teasing, coaxing more pleasure from her. London's entire body shivers.

"Do you like that, my *keeshla*?"

She nods frantically with a muffled agreement. I grin, pleased with myself, and continue thrusting into her cunt and my sensual assault on her back hole and clit. It doesn't take long before my mate is panting, her blunt claws clutching at the furs. We come together harder and faster. Her cunt clamps down on my cock and I nearly erupt. I grit my teeth until I gain control but increase my efforts to pleasure her so she reaches her peak first. I slide the tip of my finger into her puckered hole and London screams. Her body shudders.

Tension grows at the base of my spine, as does the need to give her my seed. I flick and rub her swollen clit with my tail, and once again she cries out. That triggers my own release, and I thrust hard and deep, staying rooted inside her as my own climax hits. I fill her up, not letting any of it escape. After this, the whole village will be able to smell me on her. Just the thought makes my mating marks burn.

I cover her and press soft kisses along her shoulder. When I sense her fatigue, I slip out of her cunt. She collapses in an exhausted heap on our furs. I rise and cross to the water basin to wet a cloth before returning and cleaning up my mate and then myself. London rolls to the side, and I can sense her gaze on me as I rinse the cloth out and set it on the table to be washed later. Still not ready to join the village, I lay down again facing her.

She reaches out a hand and traces the mating mark that curls and swirls over my chest near my heart. Her eyes lift to meet mine. "When I left Earth, I thought coming to Tavikh was merely the lesser of two evils. Still punishment, but not as bad as being sent to prison. My mother would have been so disappointed in me had she still been living. Except maybe your goddess got something right. Because being here with you is the best thing to ever happen to me. I have friends. I have warm clothes, and a soft bed. I don't have to go to sleep hungry at night because there isn't enough food. I feel stronger than I ever have, and like I can accomplish anything. Most importantly, I have someone who protects me and takes care of me. Maybe even…loves me the way I love him."

I cradle London's face in my hand. "You are my fated mate. My *keeshla*. You are kind and generous and brave. You are beautiful not only in body, but in spirit. How could I not love you?"

Tears well in her eyes and one spills over to slide down the side of her face and melt away beneath our furs. "Thank you for loving me."

"From now until we pass into the lands of Deeka."

The future of our village and the human settlement is uncertain, but with my Shefira at my side, we will get through anything. Together.

EPILOGUE

Remi

Escaping from the ivory-tower prison I'd been locked in my entire life had been harder than I'd expected.

But I did it.

Only took getting on a spaceship to a whole new planet to make it happen. It's been worth it though.

I stand outside the tent I share with three of my friends and breathe in the fresh Tavikhi air. Along with the scent of nature that surrounds us, is the smoky fragrance of a cooking fire. It's not quite dawn yet, and one of the two moons is still visible in the lavender sky, a color that's a far cry from Earth's blue.

The people—aliens—of our village are busy starting their day, the buzz of activity a low hum, all intent on their destination and task. Males prepare their weapons for hunting. Some of the females and a few elders, assigned to attend to this morning's meal, have gathered around the flames, getting the food ready for the entire tribe.

I stretch my arms up over my head to try and loosen the aching muscles I've acquired since coming to the Tavikhi village and joining the warriors in order to learn how to fight. My hands are slowly developing callouses after blistering so bad they bled. My gaze travels, taking in my new home. The place where I'm becoming someone different than the Remington Alcott I'd been on Earth. The place where I'm free.

Behind me, there's the sound of movement and someone pushes open the flap of our tent and steps out. I glance over my shoulder. Sage holds her crudely made coffee mug.

"Morning," she greets me, her voice slightly above a whisper. "You're up early."

"Couldn't sleep."

She comes to stand beside me. "Do you want me to ask Kyler for a tonic to help?"

I shake my head. The healer has far more important things to take care of. "I'll be okay. I think it's just because I'm afraid if I sleep, I'll wake up and this will have been nothing but a dream. I'm sure the longer we're here, the more my brain will recognize this is real and I'm not back on Earth."

"It took me a while to adjust as well, so I understand. We are here though, and this is most definitely real."

Sage has been on Tavikh longer than the rest of us, so I'll have to trust she's right.

"Okay then. I'm going to make myself some of what doesn't come close to being coffee and head to the healer's tent." She holds up her mug. "Let me know if you change your mind about the tonic."

"Thanks."

She takes off across the yellow dirt toward the central fire. Even before we arrived at the Tavikhi village less than a week ago—when we still lived in the human settlement—we were supposed to contribute to the community in some way. While I'm training to become a warrior, Sage has been Kyler's apprentice for several months. Long before Zara, Maeve, London, and I arrived on the planet.

Faint grunts and harsh smacks reach me. I walk to the other side of the village, ignoring the occasional stare from those still getting used to humans living here, and pause at the top of the hill that looks down into the training arena. Already, several warriors are sparring with each other. Long wooden staffs collide, then crash together again, while the males move with raw power and brute force. None hold back. If not for the grins on their faces, the casual observer would probably think they were trying to kill each other.

I stand there and continue to study their fighting styles, searching for any weaknesses or vulnerabilities I might be able to take advantage of. As the only female warrior—and a human one at that—the Tavikhi outweigh me by close to a hundred pounds. And even though I'm tall for a woman, they still top me by about a foot.

My gaze is drawn to one warrior in particular. He's aggressive, but also patient. He fights defensively, slowly wearing down his opponent before he strikes. Muscles upon muscles ripple beneath his purple, leathery skin that London says is butter-soft. She would know after all, considering she's married—mated—to the leader of the entire tribe.

His long, white-gold hair is pulled back into some type of braid that, if he were human, might appear feminine. Except on him, it's anything but. It only highlights his masculine face with its square-cut jaw and sharp cheek-bones. I take in the flat, bony nose and the hard ridges above yellow eyes with their dark vertical pupil that all Tavikhi possess. His grin is feral and, as though sensing his opponent's fatigue, he goes on the offensive. Strike after strike, he pushes the other male back until he sweeps the legs out from underneath his opponent and the poor, defeated male crashes onto his back, kicking up a cloud of yellow dust.

A sudden gust of wind flutters my hair around my head. I sweep it back and tuck it behind my ears. The winner leans forward with an outstretched arm to help the male on the ground, but he comes to an abrupt halt and his head jerks up. Our eyes meet and hold. There's a fluttery sensation, like a hundred butterflies have been released inside my belly. Spinning on my heels, I rush back to my tent. I reach it at the same time Zara emerges.

"Are you okay? You look spooked," she says.

I laugh, but even to my own ears it sounds forced. "Me? No, I'm fine."

She quirks her lips and gives me some serious side-eye. "If you say so. Maeve is still sleeping, so I'm going to grab us some breakfast. Wanna come?"

Since the one place I *should* be heading is the same place I just ran away from, I don't have much of a choice. Maybe a full stomach will distract me. "I could eat."

We stroll through the village to the cook fire. Sage has already left, but other tribe members come and go once they fill their bowls with whatever's on the menu. Other than occasional mornings, the only meal where the entire village eats together is in the evenings. Everyone gathers around, laughing, and trades stories of their day. It makes me feel as though I'm part of one giant family. It's nice.

A female hands Zara and I each a bowl of something that sort of resembles oatmeal. It's a bit grainy in texture, but it sticks to my insides. I add a little bit of the sap I learned comes from one of the flowering bushes here, to give it a slightly sweetened flavor. She and I head to one of the long logs that circles the central fire.

"Have you figured out what you want to do?" I ask her.

She winces. That's not good. Back on Earth, Zara came from a rich family who treated her like a doll who wasn't allowed to do anything for herself. She's been struggling with finding the right job in the village.

"While they were kind about it, the elders kicked me out of the tanning tent, which makes three tasks I've now failed at." Her shoulders droop and she pushes the mush inside her bowl around.

I gently nudge her knee with mine. "You haven't failed at anything. You just haven't found your niche yet. Don't give up. There has to be something."

Zara sighs. "I don't know what. First I was kicked out of the food prep and cooking circle. How was I supposed to know that you have to frequently stir the leburin soup or it scorches and ruins the whole thing? Plus, I almost barfed from the smell of raw dreri meat. After I gave one of the warriors a tonic that had him running to the shitter instead of helping his headache, Kyler booted me out of the healer's tent. Now this."

Poor thing has had a run of bad luck. "You're doing the best you can. That's what's important. You could always train with me, you know."

"I'd probably impale myself." Zara grimaces. "Thanks for trying to make me feel better though."

"Good morning," Maeve says quietly as she comes around to the front side of the log and sits on the ground in front of us, nearly touching our legs.

I've never met anyone as skittish as her, so she's never far from any of us. I'd actually been surprised when she agreed to come live in the village when we'd all voted on it. Granted, the vote had taken place practically during the Krijese attack on the settlement, and no one wanted to stay there alone. Not just because they were afraid either. The five of us girls are a family. We have to stick together.

Just then, the warriors crest the hill from the training arena. They rib each other good-naturedly and their laughter carries across the distance. Once again, I'm searching until I find *him*. What is it that keeps drawing me to him? He and the warrior he'd been sparring with approach. He glances in my direction several times as they are served their meal, and each time, I duck my head and focus my attention on breakfast. I've never reacted to a man like this before, let alone an alien.

Zara leans over. "Who's the hottie?"

My head jerks up and her eyes dart toward the direction where he's sitting. "Oh, just some warrior."

"Do you mean Zander's brother?" Maeve pipes up.

We both glance down at her with a questioning look. She shrugs. "What? I pay attention. If you're talking about the two guys that just sat down, then the one on the left that keeps staring at Remi is Zydon. The other one's name is Jodah, I think."

I cast a quick peek in their direction and my attention zooms in on *him*. This close, there *is* a marked resemblance between Zander and…Zydon. Didn't London say something about them being twins? Whoever he is, there's this pull that keeps tugging at me whenever he's near. It's a distraction I neither need nor want.

Thank you so much for reading!

For more Zydon and Remi, check out Fated to the Alien
Hunter

Warriors of Tavikh

Fated to the Alien Warrior
Fated to the Alien Hunter

About the Author

Erin Hale resides in the South where the summer humidity sucks the breath right out of you. She's mom to the best dog on the planet. In her free time, she enjoys reading about swoon-worthy aliens (and secretly wishes one would land on Earth) and monsters alike. She also loves traveling the globe and can be seen most often in any of the pubs in the UK—where the weather is much more acceptable—with a raspberry gin and lemonade in hand.